Jake suddenly stilled, and I realized that he'd spotted me. I felt that little jolt of awareness that I always felt when he first looked at me. I always tried to look neutral, not to let it show.

So maybe I was giving him confusing vibes, too. Maybe he was wondering, "Does she like me? Does she not? Should I make a move? Should I not?"

I really wished that I didn't feel the need to keep *everything* secret.

Read all the
MAKING A SPLASH
books!

MAKING A SPLASH #1
Robyn

MAKING A SPLASH #2
Caitlin

MAKING A SPLASH #3
Whitney

Also by Jade Parker

TO CATCH A PIRATE

MAKING A SPLASH
Whitney

JADE PARKER

Point

ISBN-13: 978-0-545-04542-1
ISBN-10: 0-545-04542-8

12 11 10 9 8 7 6 5 4 3 2 1   8 9 10 11 12 13/0

Printed in the U.S.A.
First printing, July 2008

Book design by Steve Scott

CHAPTER ONE

Working. Not exactly my idea of the perfect summer vacation. Oh, wait. Work, by defi-nition, is *not* a vacation. What *was* my dad thinking when he came up with this plan?

He was thinking I needed to experience the real world. I wasn't quite sure how a water park designed to look like a tropical island in the middle of north Texas was the *real* world, but whatever. I hadn't been able to talk him out of his insane idea. So I was trying to make the best of what I considered to be a bad situation. I mean, really, who *wants* to work during the summer? Well, okay, I had met a couple of girls who actually wanted to work — but their motivation was money. I didn't need money.

"David, don't pull all the way up to the gate," I said from the backseat of the limo as he turned into the parking lot at Paradise Falls.

He looked in the rearview mirror. Our eyes met. His brown. Mine green.

"Right, Miss Whitney," he said very formally in his really cool British accent. He brought the car to a stop, got out, jogged around, and opened the door for me.

I'd tried to get him to let me open my own door, but he'd insisted that he "simply couldn't allow that." When I was little, I liked being treated as though I were a princess. Not that I really was one. But my dad enjoyed spoiling me. Now that I was older, though, sometimes I got tired of being pampered. Makes no sense, I know, but that was how I was feeling today. Like I just wanted to be more independent than my dad and his staff would allow me to be.

"Thanks," I said. "Please don't follow."

He'd done that the first time I'd ordered him to drop me off away from the gate. He'd rolled along slowly in the car. The next time, when I'd asked him not to follow in the car, he'd walked along slightly behind me. He was good at following orders as long as they were precise. He's ex-military, British Special Forces. It's a little embarrassing to arrive at work with my very own Transporter.

Yeah, my dad is just a tad overprotective, especially when he can't be around to keep an eye on me. He's involved with a lot of international businesses so he spends quite a bit of time traveling. Usually, during the summer, I travel with him. But this summer, like I said, he'd come up with the crazy idea that I should work.

I slung my Prada tote bag over my shoulder and headed for the entrance. At the beginning of the summer, I'd tried to get here early enough that no one would witness my arrival in the embarrassing white stretch limo. My dad thought I needed a stretch so I'd have plenty of room when my friends wanted to hang out with me. I hadn't told Dad that I didn't have any friends anymore. Or at least, I hadn't had any friends until recently.

During the past two months, while working at the park, I'd been hanging around with Robyn Johnson and Caitlin Morgan. I really liked them, and they seemed to like me. Of course, there were a lot of things about me that I hadn't shared with them.

But they were starting to figure things out. When they knew everything, I knew I wouldn't be able to trust them any longer. Of course, since I wasn't telling them every-thing, maybe I didn't trust them now.

I had a horrible experience during my last school year. Someone who I thought was my best friend turned out not to be. I was hav-ing a difficult time understanding why someone would betray me. I'd gone to see a shrink for a while. My aunt Sophie, who takes care of me when Dad is away, is a big believer in shrinks. I liked Dr. Succop — unfortunate name, right? — but we really hadn't done much talking. Instead we played video games during the time I was with him. He said it was therapeutic, that it would allow me to unleash my inner demons. When Dad discovered what my sessions involved, he decided working would be better therapy and would force me to face my issues. The problem was that I wasn't really sure what my issues were.

People were already lined up at the ticket booths, waiting for the park to open. *Get a life*, I thought as I swiped my park ID through the security lock at the employee entrance. Maybe I was just jealous. I didn't see anyone standing in line who looked like he or she was alone. Everyone seemed to have someone to share his or her day with. Friends, buddies, family. Not being alone a good deal of the time was a foreign concept for me.

My mom died from cancer a couple of years ago. I didn't like to think about her being gone. I still missed her a lot. My therapist assured me that it was typical, that I would always miss her. So at least when it came to grief, I was apparently normal. But when it came to friends . . .

I'd had some close friends, only they turned out to be my worst enemies. Maybe they were the issue that I needed to deal with, because now I was wary of making friends, of trusting people not to have ulterior motives where I was concerned. Everyone wanted something from me, even if that something was just to make me look bad.

The gate clicked open. I walked through.

"Hey, Whitney," the guard said. All he needed was a beard and he could fill in for Santa Claus. As a matter of fact, maybe he did in December when Paradise Falls was closed. The park management hired several retirees who were just looking to fill their days — mostly because many of the positions didn't provide much advancement. Since the guard received free passes to the water park, he was a big hit with his grandkids.

"Hey, Mr. Smith."

"How's your dad?"

"He's good. He's in Paris this week."

"I went to Paris once," he said. "Lovely city. Great food."

"Yeah, I liked it, too." I'd been to several foreign cities. I had a world map on my computer. I colored in each country when I traveled to it. I tapped my gold Cartier watch. "I'd better get to work."

"Have fun."

I never understood why he said that. Who had fun working? The two words simply didn't go together.

I brushed past him and walked along the cement path that led to the main portion of the park. I slowed as I approached the park's mascot. The green-and-yellow parrot was supposed to welcome everyone who walked by.

"*Brawk!* Daddy's girl! *Brawk!*"

"Don't call me that." Who knew parrots could recognize people? I'd spent some time watching the trainer, Mitch, teach the bird what he needed to say. "Welcome to Paradise Falls!" Mitch had thought teaching him to say "Daddy's girl" was cute. At the time, so did I, but then I hadn't planned on ever walking past the bird at the park. Now, the words were just a little embarrassing. Thank goodness, no other employees were around. I didn't want to explain what was going on with the bird. I tossed a treat up to him to shut him up.

Then I headed for the employee locker rooms. I wasn't really fond of locker rooms. No matter how clean they were, they always smelled like old dirty socks. Ours also smelled like chlorine, which made sense since we were a water park and an abundance of chlorine and other chemicals were running through the systems.

Even though I'd started to like being here, I set my expression to just-too-bored-to-care. I'd learned the hard way to never let people know what I was really thinking, and never, ever let them know what I was feeling. Psyched for a day of not being the real me, I pushed open the door, removed my Dior sunglasses, and sauntered in.

Many of the girl employees were already there, changing into their uniforms. The lifeguards and ride attendants wore red bathing suits and visors. Those who worked away from the water, like I did, wore red shorts, a white polo shirt with the Paradise Falls logo, and a red visor. No one was spared the red visor. Apparently fashion sense wasn't important at places designed for amusement.

"Hey, Whitney," Robyn said, smiling at me. Her brown hair was pulled back into a ponytail. Everyone with long hair had to wear it in a boring ponytail. I did it only when someone reminded me. Otherwise, I left my blond hair to brush over my shoulders. I wore it loose to be rebellious, a small statement that I really didn't want to be here. So far I hadn't gotten in trouble. Chances were that I wouldn't. We had only a month to go before the park closed down for the off-season. Ninety percent of the park's employees were students. When we were in school, we weren't available to work.

"You're usually here before us," Robyn added.

"Us" was Robyn and her best friend, Caitlin, who was pulling off her T-shirt. She wore her bathing suit underneath her clothes. She tossed her tee into her locker and used her fingers to fluff her short black hair. Short hair looks good on certain people. It looked good on Caitlin and brought out the deep blue of her eyes. I was almost jealous because her eyes were such a startling hue, but then mine were a vibrant green.

"Yeah, so what's up with that?" Caitlin asked.

Shrugging, I punched in the key code to my locker. No way was I going to tell them that I'd stayed up way too late last night thinking about Jake, so I'd overslept this morning. Jake worked at the park, too. He was assigned to one of the ice-cream carts. Basically, he loaded ice cream into the cart, set it up where they told him to, and sold ice cream. It was funny, because for most of the summer he'd been assigned to spots near wherever I happened to be working, so we'd gotten to know each other a little.

We had a strange sort of relationship. I liked him. I liked him a *lot*. Sometimes we palled around together, but it always seemed to be by accident. He never really acted like he was interested in me. But he always seemed to be there when I needed something.

Like I said, strange. I really couldn't figure us out. And I was feeling a little bit of pressure to define our relationship. If he didn't want to be more than friends, then I might have to start looking at other guys for what I wanted — which was my first kiss.

Since I'd met Robyn and Caitlin, they'd each acquired a boyfriend. Robyn's boyfriend, Sean Morgan, had started out the summer as our supervisor when she and I had worked in the kiddie zone, officially known as Mini Falls. Sean was also Caitlin's brother. Caitlin was dating Michael Romeo. He brought his twin brothers to the park nearly every day. Michael always hung around Tsunami, which was where Caitlin was a lifeguard, so they'd met there.

Tsunami was the signature pool of the park with twelve-foot waves. Totally awesome.

Before this summer, I would have been like Michael — lying around in the sun, soaking up the rays, playing in the human-generated surf.

Instead, I was helping out with Parties and Entertainment. Such an unimaginative name, but it summed up exactly what we did. I'd moved to P&E — as those in the know called it — because I didn't like doing anything lifeguard-intensive: watching kids, being responsible if they got hurt. Parties were all about fun. No CPR was involved. Kids didn't nearly drown in cake. They might eat too much and get sick, but that wasn't my problem. That was the domain of the park cleanup crew.

I always enjoyed throwing parties. Sometimes I would pretend that the ones at the park were my personal parties and that everyone was there to be with me — because they liked me — not because of who my dad was. James St. Clair was rich, powerful, able to do just about anything he wanted. We lived a sweet life. Dad worked hard for it, though. Sometimes people don't understand that money doesn't grow on trees. At least it doesn't in our yard.

I'd been really careful about making sure that the people I worked with didn't know who my dad was. Oh, the park's general manager, Mr. T, and a few of the office staff knew. But the kids who worked in the park — the lifeguards, ride attendants, clerks, cooks, ice-cream guys — didn't know. I knew if they found out, they'd treat me differently. Everyone always did.

I'd actually never planned for them to find out that my family had a lot of money, but that information sort of slipped out over the summer. I tried to pass my designer stuff off as knockoffs, but most of the employees didn't believe it. Then there was the whole arriving-at-work-in-a-limo thing. Really spoiled the poor girl image.

"Just wanted to sleep late," I said, brushing off Caitlin's question and my reason for being late, like it was no big deal.

"You pretty much get to do anything you want, don't you?" Caitlin asked.

Robyn and I had hit it off shortly after we met. Robyn was quiet, the kind of person who wants everyone to be happy. Caitlin was a little more outgoing, a little more in your face. Or at least she was in *my* face. Nosy, too. She hated not knowing what was going on. For a while, she had threatened to Google me if I didn't spill my secrets. But since I'd been instrumental in her getting together with Michael, she'd backed off.

Michael's father owned a laser light-show company, and I'd convinced the general manager to hire them to put on a show for our Fourth of July extravaganza. Caitlin had been on my entertainment team, so she'd gotten to know Michael. Now she owed me, so I was safe from her Googling me. A search on my name could bring up some pretty embarrassing stuff.

"Pretty much," I said.

Caitlin and I were a little closer to being friends, but just a little. We both liked to be in charge. Since I didn't have any brothers or sisters, I was used to doing what I wanted, when I wanted. Caitlin had a brother, but she still got her way. I guess she'd learned to fight for what she wanted.

"See y'all at lunch," Caitlin said.

"You're not having lunch with Michael?" I asked. She usually did.

"No. One of his brothers has an ear infection. Too much time in the pool, so they're taking a couple of days off."

"His brother could come to the park and not go in the water."

"Yeah, right. Have you ever tried to control a rambunctious boy?"

"Babysitting is not my thing." That was part of the reason I stopped being a lifeguard: way too much responsibility. I thought it was much better to be in a position that was all about partying.

"Well, taking him to a water park and telling him not to get into the water would be like taking you to a mall and telling you not to buy something."

I grinned. The one thing Caitlin and I had in common was our love of shopping. Still, I was a little insulted that she thought my willpower was so weak. "I could go to a mall and not buy anything."

She laughed. "Yeah, right. When global warming is reversed."

"I could resist buying longer than you could."

"Wanna bet?" she asked.

"Yeah."

She grinned at me, issuing her challenge. "Day off. The mall. Right when it opens. Loser has to buy the winner a new pair of shoes."

"You two are crazy," Robyn said. "Who issues a shopping challenge?"

"Maybe it'll be the start of a new reality TV show," Caitlin said, before looking back at me. "So is it a bet?"

Grinning, I stuck out my hand. "It's a bet."

Caitlin and I shook. "Sucker," she said in a low voice before turning to walk off.

No, I wasn't. Even if I lost — which I was certain I wouldn't — I'd still win. I now had something to do on my day off. Something to do *with* someone. I wouldn't be hanging out all by myself — which had been my original option. Quite honestly, me by myself wasn't very much fun.

"That was insane," Robyn said, adjusting her visor.

"It'll be entertaining." I was already wearing my uniform so I stuffed my tote into the locker.

"Are you sure everything is okay?" Robyn asked.

"Sure. Why wouldn't it be?"

"I don't know. You just seem distracted or something."

I wanted to tell her about my confusion regarding Jake. I really did. She was the first one of us to get a boyfriend. She might be able to give me some tips or at least explain what signs to look for so I'd know if Jake liked me the way that I liked him.

But I hesitated. Did I think she was going to sell my story to *Teen People*? "Whitney St. Clair's Crush!"

I worried because it had happened before. Marci Spencer — someone who I once thought was my best friend — had sold a picture of me to a teen gossip rag. During Thanksgiving, Dad and I had been serving food to the homeless at a shelter. A good thing, right? But the caption had read "Whitney St. Clair gets a taste of real life."

It was mean. I'd gotten a taste of real life when my mom died.

Then my supposed friend Marci had captured me on video dancing at a party. She'd posted it on YouTube. "Could Whitney St. Clair be the next winner of *Dancing with the Stars*? You vote!"

I was mortified, because it was obvious that she was mocking me. I looked pretty awful dancing. I was jerky and uncoordinated. In the background, some people were pointing and laughing. I hadn't noticed them at the time. I hadn't noticed Marci recording me either. I learned everything when the video was plastered all over the Internet.

My dad advised me to ignore people with small minds, people who focused on little things, people who were petty. I discovered that meant ignoring all the friends I had at the time because they were all petty: Marci Spencer, Andi Yeager, Sandi Kennedy. When I'd been part of the group, Marci insisted that I spell my name Whitni. Our motto was "The i's have eyes."

It had meant that we were gossip central. We each had a MySpace page and posted things on the Internet. We revealed secrets, no matter how hurtful they were. We'd get together and laugh about how much we had embarrassed someone. We gave awards for the most devastating comment. No one was safe from us. Not even those within our own group, as it turned out.

So now I found it difficult to trust. Robyn wasn't anything like Marci. I knew that. But still, I wasn't sure that she wouldn't become like Marci, if she ever found out the truth about me.

"I'm totally fine," I assured her.

We were ready for work so we walked out of the employee locker rooms together. Since we were both wearing sunglasses, I couldn't see her brown eyes. When I can't see someone's eyes, I always have a hard time knowing what they're thinking. But I also felt safer, more protected when I was wearing mine, so I took a chance. "How did you know that Sean liked you?" I asked.

Robyn laughed lightly, like she was embarrassed. "I didn't. Not until he kissed me."

That wasn't much help. Jake had never even *tried* to kiss me. He didn't talk to me much. He seemed to just watch me more than anything. Not in a weird stalker kind of way. More like he was trying to figure me out. I didn't know if that was good or not.

"He didn't even hint?" I asked.

She laughed a little more loudly. "I think he did. I was just too . . . I don't know . . . stupid, I guess, to notice."

Okay, this was a little more helpful. I tried to remember how my therapist had attempted to trick me into answering questions before he'd discovered that I was no longer trickable and we'd started playing video games.

"I don't think you were being stupid. If you didn't know they were hints then how would you know that they meant anything? What's an example?"

"He brought me ice cream when I was on break."

Huh. Jake gave me ice cream, but I didn't think it meant anything. He was one of the guys with an ice-cream cart. He gave ice cream to many employees. It was one of our perks. We got free ice cream when we were on break.

"What else?" I asked.

"He just always seemed to be there."

Jake was always there, but again, I thought it was part of his job. I worked in P&E, so I oversaw a lot of birthday parties. The park provided the ice cream for those parties, and Jake was the one who brought the ice cream over. He'd stay around and help out. But I wasn't sure that I was the reason he stayed. I think it was his job to hang around.

"Are you wondering about Jake?" Robyn asked.

I stumbled to a stop. "Why would you think that?"

She grinned. "Come on, Whitney. I see the way y'all look at each other."

"And how's that?"

"Like maybe you like each other."

I shook my head, because I suspected she wasn't good at reading people. "I don't know, Robyn. I'm not so sure he likes me."

"He does. He's always around you. Besides, you're so nice. How can he not like you?"

"I know it's difficult to believe, but not everyone likes me." I sighed. "He may be one of them. He doesn't usually talk to me. He's just kinda *there*."

"So, maybe you should just ask him."

"Ask him?"

"Yeah, ask him if he likes you."

If he said no, it would hurt too much. I'd be mortified. "Would you have asked Sean?"

"No way! Even when I started to like him, I was afraid he didn't like me." She wrinkled her nose. "I guess that's where you are, huh?"

"Yeah, I guess. Does he like me? Does he not? I totally don't know."

"I could ask Sean to ask him —"

"No!" I exclaimed before she'd even finished with that crazy idea. "I don't want people to know that I like Jake. If they know and he doesn't like me, I'll just be more embarrassed. So don't tell anyone, okay?"

"Sean wouldn't tell anyone, except me. And I'd tell you. It would be a small circle."

But I knew that circles could grow, like throwing a rock in water. The circle just got wider and wider and wider. "I really don't want anyone else involved."

She shrugged. "Okay. I'll respect that."

"Thanks."

We were at the part of the park where the main offices were. "I'll see you at lunch," I told her.

"Okay." She headed off toward Mini Falls.

I wandered over to the office building. It really looked out of place. No thatched roof, no sand leading to the door. No palm trees. Maybe everyone inside wanted to be taken seriously.

I opened the door and was hit with a blast of air-conditioning. That was another thing about the office that was so un-tropical island. They kept it Antarctica-freezing in there. I knew the truth of that because Dad and I had gone on a three-week cruise to Antarctica. Not that the cruise ship had stayed there very long. Just long enough for us to set foot on the continent at the bottom of the world, so we could say we'd done it and I could color in an entire continent on my map.

I went to the P&E office. Charlotte was the permanent full-time entertainment manager, which meant that she stayed on staff year-round planning things that would happen during summer, like the season opening and special days. She was at her desk, talking on the phone, making notes. Probably taking reservations for a party.

I walked over to the main white board on the wall that listed the parties coming in today. We had only two birthday parties. The first started at eleven, right when the park opened. I smiled. I'd begin my work shift with Jake. Maybe if I paid more attention, I could figure out if he was trying to send me signals.

I heard Charlotte hang up and turned to face her. She smiled brightly. "Good morning."

"Hey. Is Lisa already at the pavilion?" I asked. Lisa was the summer supervisor. She was a freshman in college. I liked working with her, mostly because she was a control freak, which might sound like a bad thing, but she did all the work. She didn't trust anyone else to make it perfect, so I got to do the fun stuff, like greet the guests at the gate, escort them to the pavilion designated for their party, and take pictures. Pretty much anything I wanted.

"Yes, she is."

"I'll head over there, then." I turned to go.

"One sec."

I looked back over my shoulder and smiled. "What's up?"

"As soon as y'all get the second birthday party cleared away, I want to see both of you back in my office. I just took a reservation for a huge affair. The Spencers have rented the park after hours this coming Sunday for their daughter's sixteenth birthday. They want a luau —"

She was still talking about the luau and what the Spencers wanted, but all I heard was a loud rushing in my ears. The same rushing I heard when I took an inner tube down the raging rapids that were part of the river that circled the park. Spencer was a common name. It couldn't be —

"What's their daughter's name?" I finally dared to ask.

"Marci. With an *i*. Mrs. Spencer was really insistent about that. That we spell everything correctly." She stopped talking and stood up. "Are you all right, Whitney? You look like you're going to be sick."

"I'm fine. I gotta go help Lisa."

I walked out of the office, out of the building, into the heat of early August, but I was still cold.

The *i*'s have eyes were coming to the water park. All my secrets were about to be revealed.

CHAPTER TWO

I thought about not going to help out with today's birthday parties. I considered going back to the locker room, getting my cell phone out of my tote bag, calling David, and telling him to come pick me up. I contemplated quitting.

Instead, I walked to the pavilion in Mini Falls where the first birthday party of the morning was being set up. Twelve little monsters would soon descend on us. As far as the amount of work involved, this morning we didn't have much. Sometimes we had as many as eight parties going at one time, and some of them had a lot more than a dozen guests.

I saw Jake standing inside the pavilion. He was using the helium canister to blow up the balloons that would be tied to the table reserved for our party guests.

I stopped walking and just watched him. He had auburn hair that he kept buzzed short. It made him look like maybe he should attend a military academy. A lot of the guys — and even some girls — who worked at the park kept their hair short. We were outside most of the time and it was hot. Besides, visors messed up any other kind of hairstyle.

But it wasn't only Jake's hair that made him look as though he might salute you at any minute. He was also in shape. When he dipped ice cream, the muscles in his arms actually bulged a little. He had dark brown eyes that were almost black. And the longest black eyelashes. It was wrong for a guy to have eyelashes that long. I'd stared at his eyelashes, his eyes, and him a lot when he didn't realize it.

It was really a little pathetic, because I enjoyed studying him and trying to figure him out. I knew he had a tiny scar on his chin. I didn't know how he got it. I knew that when he smiled, one side of his mouth curled up a little higher than the other. I knew he had an almost perfect smile, except for one front tooth that slightly crossed over the other one, as though maybe he'd once worn braces but hadn't been good about wearing his retainer once he got them off. He just looked like the kind of guy who wouldn't always follow the rules, who wouldn't always do what he was supposed to.

I put on a show, pretended that I was rebellious and didn't always do what I was told, but the truth was that I *always* did what was expected of me. That's the reason I was at the pavilion now: because it was my job to help with this stupid birthday party. Knowing that Marci was coming, suddenly everything seemed lame.

At the beginning of the summer, I worked at Splash, a really safe and unexciting slide in Mini Falls. When I told Mr. T that I wanted to work in Parties and Entertainment, he moved me with no questions asked. So now I needed to move someplace else, so I wouldn't be around for this dumb luau. It probably would be a lot of fun to arrange, if not for the person that it was being planned for. I needed to figure out where to move. It had to be someplace where I wouldn't be visible to the i's.

Jake suddenly stilled, and I realized that he'd spotted me. I felt that little jolt of awareness that I always felt when he first looked at me. I always tried to look neutral, not to let it show. So maybe I was giving him confusing vibes, too. Maybe he was wondering, "Does she like me? Does she not? Should I make a move? Should I not?"

I really wished that I didn't feel the need to keep *everything* secret. I wished I could just be me, without worrying about getting hurt or being taken advantage of.

The bells echoed through the park signaling that the gates were opening. The madness was about to start.

Jake grinned. "Hey, you're a little late to

help." He carried the balloons to a table and attached them through a hole designed to keep the balloons tethered at the end of the table.

"I was busy," I lied. "Where's Lisa?"

"She left to get the birthday guests."

"Oh." That was my job, but since I hadn't been around she'd had to do it. It wasn't my fault, though. If Charlotte hadn't detained me so she could tell me about this great birthday party that we'd be hosting, I would have been there sooner.

Then I had a crazy thought. *What if Marci invited me to this insane party?* She was bound to invite just about everyone who went to the private school we attended. Yes, she was probably inviting the whole school. Why else would her parents rent the entire water park?

With each thought, this situation was getting worse. Survival seemed impossible.

"Are you okay?" Jake asked.

"Why is everyone asking me that today?"

He rolled his shoulders. "I didn't know everyone was. Maybe you just look like something is wrong. So what's up?"

I really wanted to tell him about Marci and the i's. I wanted to ask if he liked me. Instead I said, "Just bored working here. I'm thinking that I want to work somewhere else."

"What? You mean, like work at some other water park?"

He sounded seriously disappointed. That was a good sign, right? He wanted me to be here.

"No, just work someplace else around here."

"Like where?"

"I don't know." I sat on the metal bench of the metal picnic table. Metal was easy to keep clean. Just spray it down with a water hose at the end of the day.

Jake sat beside me. "Really, Whitney, what's wrong?"

He sounded genuinely concerned. That was another good sign . . . I think. Or maybe he just cared about everyone. Still, I couldn't tell him about the i's without telling him about me. I wanted him to like me without knowing everything about me. Was that even possible?

The party pavilion was in Mini Falls, near the Lost Lagoon, which was a shallow pool with a fake wrecked pirate ship in its center. Lifeguards were standing around. Kids, along with their parents, were starting to make their way to the area. No unsupervised children were allowed in this area of the park.

I thought about what Robyn said about Sean being there whenever she needed him. I needed someone. And Jake was there. But did it mean anything? How could I figure it out without actually asking him?

I needed some way to test his interest in me, something that would tell me what his feelings were.

"Some of us are going out for pizza after work. Do you want to go with us?" I heard myself asking, without thinking it through.

"That's the reason you're acting funny and thinking of working someplace else? Because you're going out for pizza?"

"I've got a lot on my mind. So do you want to go out for pizza or not?" I knew I sounded put out. Why would he be interested in me when I was so difficult? I had a feeling that he was going to fail this test. And it wouldn't be his fault. I was a whiz at taking tests but lousy at giving them.

"Sure," he said.

I almost hugged him, but it would have been so uncool to let on how excited I was that he'd said yes. So maybe he did like me. I grinned.

"I love pizza. So which place?" he asked.

Or maybe he just wanted the pizza. I really should have given this plan more thought before putting it into action.

"Uh, I forgot to ask where we're going. I'll let you know later today."

We heard shrieks and looked over. Lisa was leading a dozen or so kiddos and their parents over to the pavilion.

"Looks like it's showtime," Jake said.

For now. The real show, though, would be later tonight. Maybe then I'd have a chance to figure out what our relationship was: coworkers, friends, or more?

"Pizza? You want to go out for pizza tonight?" Caitlin asked.

Robyn, Caitlin, and I met at the Tsunami lounging deck for lunch. The area was covered in sand, at least twelve inches deep, so guests had the sense that they were on a tropical beach. The perfect place to host a luau. But I didn't want to think about that upcoming nightmare. After the luau, I had a feeling I'd have nothing but bad memories of this place.

"Yeah." I was stretched out on the lounge chair, trying to look like nothing mattered. "I sorta invited Jake to go out for pizza but I made it sound like it was a group of people, so now I need a group of people. So are you interested?"

"That is so Whitney," Caitlin said. "You

36

make plans and assume people are going to do what you want."

My aunt called me a little dictator. All I had to do was say what I wanted to do and we did it. Since my mom died, no one in the family told me no. I was poor little Whitney, and people didn't want me to be sad. So yeah, a lot of times I planned things without thinking them through. But it always worked out somehow.

"Is that a problem for you?" I asked. "Because I can un-invite you." The words were just talk. I really wanted Robyn and Caitlin to be there. They were the closest thing I had to friends. Since they had boyfriends, if I had questions or needed someone to guide me, they would be the best ones to seek advice from. Like a lifeline on *Who Wants to be a Millionaire*. I just needed help in figuring all this possible-boyfriend stuff out.

"It's not a problem. It's just weird," Caitlin said. "The way you try to control everything."

"So are you in?" I asked, ready to move on to the next problem on my list.

"We're in," Robyn said.

I knew she'd agree to it without giving me a hard time. Maybe if I told Caitlin about my doubts regarding Jake, she'd be a little more enthusiastic about coming along tonight.

"Sure, we're in," Caitlin said.

She didn't complain that Robyn had spoken for her. She only complained about things that I did. My relationship with her was almost as confusing as the one I had with Jake. Is she my friend or isn't she? I was pretty sure she was.

"I'll call Michael," she continued. "He should be able to come. So where are we going?"

"Uh, well, I don't know. I hadn't gotten that far with my plan."

Caitlin laughed. "You invited us for pizza and you don't know where we're going?"

I didn't like her laughing at me. I knew it was because she didn't know the entire story, so I felt compelled to explain. "If you want to know the truth, it was a test for Jake."

"A test?"

She was surprised by the test, but not about Jake? Had Robyn said something to her or had she figured it out, too? I decided that she probably figured it out. She was pretty observant, which was one reason that she made such a good lifeguard and had saved a kid's life. So if both Robyn and Caitlin figured it out, why couldn't I? I was embarrassed to admit the truth. "I don't know if Jake likes me, so I thought if I invited him to do something with me, it would help me figure it out. If he liked me, he'd say yes. If he didn't, he'd make up some excuse about being busy."

"Huh. That kinda makes sense I guess," Caitlin said. "So you asked, he said yes, so you know he likes you."

I shrugged. "Actually, I don't know. I thought the plan was foolproof, but then he said that he loves pizza. What if he was just saying yes because of the pizza?"

"So you should have invited him to do something that he normally wouldn't want to do," Caitlin said.

"I guess. But I don't know what that is. We don't talk that much."

"I could have Michael just ask him if he likes you."

I rolled my eyes. Was involving their boyfriends everyone's solution to my problem? Why not just use the park's announcement system? "No, I don't want to get more people involved. Just help me figure out where to go tonight."

"Pizza Palace," Robyn suggested. "It's near where we live. It's got more than pizza. It's got games, so if it gets awkward at the table and you can't think of anything to talk about, you can always go play something."

"You think it'll get awkward? You think this was a stupid idea?"

"No, I don't think it was stupid. I also don't think he agreed because of the pizza."

I wished I was as sure.

"I'll have Sean go on MapQuest and print you a map before we leave," Robyn said.

Sean worked in marketing now so he spent a lot of his time in the front offices. He had his own computer for designing marketing stuff. Sometimes we passed in the hallway when I was on my way to the P&E office.

"Thanks, but I just need the address. The limo has a navigation system." Besides, David was pretty good about figuring out where things were.

"Okay. I'll get it for you," Robyn said.

Robyn and I had bonded earlier in the summer when we chased off some bullies. Later we rescued a child who nearly drowned. She performed CPR, while telling me what to do to help. But I let her take all the credit because I knew a TV interview scenario when I saw it, and I didn't want to appear on TV. I hadn't wanted the i's to see me and know I was working here.

On the Fourth of July, Caitlin had saved

a boy from choking, with no help from anyone. She and Robyn were now both designated park heroines.

So while I'd helped Robyn, I hadn't really done anything to make me stand out — not the way Robyn and Caitlin had. What was I going to do? Save a kid from a popping balloon?

I wasn't jealous of their accomplishments. But the two people who were the closest to being my friends had boyfriends now and had done something at their jobs to make them an important part of the water park. I was feeling like a total loser. I knew it was my fault because I hadn't taken working here seriously. Oh, I'd planned a party for the employees and arranged a light show for the Fourth of July, but it wasn't as though I'd averted a crisis.

Add to that the fact that I was lonely since I'd discovered I had no true friends at my old school and was suddenly outnumbered by people who *were* making a difference, and I was getting a taste of the real world my dad had been talking about. I didn't like it much.

I shifted on the lounge chair and cleared my throat. "Okay, I have one other little problem."

Robyn sat up as though she'd been waiting for this moment, as though she'd known that eventually I'd break down and confess everything. "What's that?"

"Sunday, there's going to be this big birthday bash for someone I know. They're renting the water park after hours."

"Isn't that, like, mega-expensive?" Caitlin asked.

"They're mega-rich."

"I think it's cool that your friends want to have a party here," Robyn said.

"They're not my friends," I admitted. "They used to be, but well, they're like Jasmine except they're much, much worse."

Jasmine was an employee who worked one of the slides. She'd stolen away Caitlin's first guy, Tanner, then tried to steal Michael from her, too. But Michael had been way more interested in Caitlin than in Jasmine. So now he and Caitlin were together.

"They stole a guy from you?" Caitlin asked.

"No. I've never had a guy —"

"You've got Jake," Caitlin said.

"We don't know that. My test was seriously flawed. Anyway, they call themselves the i's. Marci, Andi, and Sandi, because their names all end in i's."

"The i's? So how old are they? Four?" Caitlin asked.

I smiled. I should have known Caitlin would think they were as silly as I now did. Sometimes we did connect.

"The thing is, with the party being here, I'm going to have to help with it, which means that they'll see me —"

"Are you embarrassed that they'll find out we're your friends?" Robyn asked.

"What? No! Why would you think that?"

"Well, you're rich, obviously, and they're rich. Caitlin and I aren't. Obviously."

"Money has nothing to do with this. They're complete jerks. They do mean things. I just don't want to be involved with them. Being around them — I know it'll be a disaster."

"So tell Charlotte," Caitlin said. "You always get what you want around here anyway. Tell her you don't want to work on this party. I'll bet she'll let you out of it."

I sat up, leaned forward, and tugged on the hem of my shorts. "I guess I could do that."

It was a simple solution that might just work. But something about it bothered me. I just couldn't figure out what.

"I think that's a really bad idea," Robyn said.

"Why?" I asked.

"You're letting them win. You like doing parties. And if they're renting the entire park, after hours, then it's going to be an awesome

45

event. Are you telling me that you don't want to be involved in making it happen?"

Did she have to be so right? The park was large enough that I might not even run into them. And I liked working in parties and entertainment. I just needed to find a way to avoid Marci. I could help plan the party — which she was also right about. A luau would be awesome to arrange. I just wouldn't be around when it actually took place. Or I'd find a way to work behind the scenes. Easy, no problem.

"I can't let her win," I said. "You're right," I added begrudgingly.

"Of course I am. I'm always right." She grinned and scooted over on her lounge chair until our knees were almost touching. "Now we just need to concentrate on tonight, on figuring out if Jake likes you."

"How much do you like him?" Caitlin asked.

I studied Caitlin. I didn't see anything mean or conniving in her expression. Of course, with her wearing sunglasses it was difficult to be sure. But I was tired of watching everything I did, everything I said. I was weary of trying to protect myself, of keeping up shields. I took a deep breath and blurted out the truth. "I like him a whole lot."

She punched the air. "I knew it!"

My stomach knotted up. "What are you going to do with the information?"

She tilted her head slightly, like a confused dog would. "Help you get together with him."

"Oh. Really?"

"Well, yeah. If it wasn't for you, I probably wouldn't be dating Michael now, so I sorta owe you. But even if I didn't, that's what friends do. Help each other."

It was a novel concept for me and made me a little nervous.

"Okay. Great." I had never looked so forward to eating pizza in my life.

CHAPTER THREE

The park closed at eight. We all agreed to meet at the Pizza Palace at nine. I didn't have much time to go home and change. But I did the best I could. I took a quick shower. I dried my hair and left it hanging loose, brushing my shoulders. I applied mascara to my eyelashes, a hint of blush to my cheeks, and just a touch of eye shadow. Because I wasn't allowed to have makeup yet — Dad thought I was too young — I sneaked everything I needed out of Aunt Sophie's cosmetic case. She wouldn't miss anything. Her cosmetic case came on wheels because she used so much and hauled it all wherever she went.

I changed into a denim skirt. I double-layered a red spaghetti-strap tank top over a white one. I put on a red-and-blue choker that had a touch of silver, and slipped on some denim wedge sandals that I knew would have Caitlin drooling. She was all about the shoes. I tossed all my stuff — wallet, cell phone, brush, etc. — into an Armani leather tote. Then I hurried down the stairs.

I planned to concentrate on Jake and ignore the disaster of Marci that was looming on the horizon. I figured that since the party was only a few days away, Marci would be sending out e-vites. I quickly checked my e-mail when I'd gotten home. Nothing. I was more relieved than hurt. Her not inviting me saved me the trouble of coming up with an excuse for not attending. Of course, I'd still be there — just in the shadows.

During our meeting that afternoon, Charlotte had emphasized that she expected every P&E team member to be there on

Sunday, pulling her weight. She might not have been imaginative, but she was smart. She recognized demanding customers when she talked to them on the phone.

By the time I reached the bottom of the stairs, I was so tense that I thought I could snap in two. I didn't want to think about Sunday. I just wanted to enjoy tonight, being with Jake. I wanted to figure out what, if anything, was between us.

"Where are you heading?" Aunt Sophie asked.

I squeaked and stubbed my toe on the marble floor as I staggered to a stop. I was so absorbed worrying about Marci and the party that I hadn't noticed my aunt standing in the doorway that led to the living room. She wore a silk lounging outfit. Her white-blond hair was pulled back and held in place with an expensive jeweled clip. She was holding Westie, my little dog.

She was totally glamorous. I didn't understand why she wasn't married. As far as I knew, she didn't even have a boyfriend.

"I thought I told you," I said, catching my breath and hoping my heart rate would return to normal. "I'm meeting some friends at the Pizza Palace."

I *had* told her, but it was sort of a hit-and-run telling. I'd mentioned it as I hurried to my room earlier, hoping she would catch just enough to know I was going out, not enough to feel that she needed to give me the third degree and gather all the details for Dad. If I was too young to wear makeup, I knew Dad would think I was too young to have a boyfriend.

Now Aunt Sophie was furrowing her brow and shifting into what I recognized as her *Law & Order* stance. "Who are these friends?"

"I work with them at Paradise Falls."

She tapped her French-manicured finger on Westie's nose. His little pink tongue darted out and licked her finger. "Is that Jake boy going to be there?"

She'd met Jake when I had a small party at the house just before the Fourth of July. I helped arrange the park's laser light show, so I invited everyone who was involved for a sneak peek. I couldn't tell from Aunt Sophie's voice if she thought Jake being at the pizza place was a good thing or a bad thing — so I wasn't exactly sure how to answer: with the absolute truth or a version of the truth that wouldn't get me in trouble if it was discovered.

I decided on the truth. "Maybe."

I mean, honestly, there was always a chance he wouldn't show.

She nodded. "Okay. Have fun."

She strolled back into the living room. Just like that. She was letting me go. I couldn't believe it had been that easy. Even knowing a guy was going to be there, she hadn't objected. Jake must have made a really favorable impression on her. *Huh*. I didn't even remember them talking.

But I wasn't going to question her. Maybe, unlike Dad, she recognized that I was grow-ing up. Or maybe she just wanted to get back to her favorite TV program. Whatever.

I rushed outside where David was waiting with the limo. I had given him the address earlier, so I just clambered inside, took my seat, and buckled up.

The Pizza Palace wasn't much of a palace. Little colorful flags waved from atop some pathetic spires that I guessed were meant to represent a castle. When I got inside, I walked over a wooden drawbridge and through an archway into the food area. I saw Robyn, Sean, Caitlin, and Michael sitting at a round table. I glanced around. I didn't see Jake. I would be mortified if he didn't show.

I walked over to the table and took one of the empty chairs. "Hey, sorry I'm late."

"Actually, I think we were early," Sean said. Like his sister, Caitlin, he had dark hair and the bluest eyes I'd ever seen. He also had a killer smile, which he flashed at me.

I'd liked him the minute he introduced himself as my supervisor my first day working at the water park. I was nervous and he assured me that everything would be just fine. He promised that I would enjoy working with Robyn. He was a terrific supervisor and a nice guy. He and Robyn seemed perfect for each other.

I also liked Michael as soon as I met him. He had dark hair and the most fascinating silver eyes. The first time I spoke to him, I found myself distracted by his eyes. I enjoyed talking with him, but it was pretty obvious from the start that he was interested in Caitlin. He asked me a lot of questions about her. I didn't know many of the answers, but it didn't seem to matter to him. I'd known the answer to the most important question: at the time she didn't have a boyfriend. I was glad that he was dating her now. Even if it meant that I was the only one without a boyfriend.

Sean lifted the pitcher of root beer and poured some into a frosty mug. Then he pushed it toward me. He was a take-charge kind of guy.

"We were waiting to order the pizza until everyone got here," he said.

"We're expecting one more, right?" Michael asked.

"Yeah," I said. "Jake. You know him, don't you?"

"I think so. The ice-cream guy, right?"

"That makes it sound like he's made out of ice cream," I said. I hated labels.

Caitlin laughed. "Sorry, I just think of him that way because he works the ice-cream cart."

Michael winked at Caitlin, and I wondered what she'd told him about Jake and my interest in him. Probably everything. Not that it mattered. It was probably pretty obvious anyway — otherwise, we wouldn't all be sitting there waiting for him.

I glanced around again. I had never been here before. Kids were jumping around in an inflatable castle. Tunnels and slides ended at a large sandbox-looking thing filled with foam balls to cushion the landing. Skee-ball alleys and video game machines were arranged along the walls. It appeared that the Pizza Palace competed with Paradise Falls for birthday parties, because several tables were reserved for groups, and at one table the birthday kid wore a paper crown.

I wondered where Jake was.

I suddenly felt very uncomfortable. I arranged this little outing and it was slipping completely out of my control. I turned my attention back to those at my table. "Maybe we should go ahead and order."

I didn't want to say it out loud, but I was beginning to think that Jake wasn't coming. Maybe he didn't know how to say "not interested" in person.

"Sorry I'm late."

I nearly jumped out of my skin as the chair next to me scraped across the floor. Then Jake was sitting beside me. He had changed his clothes, too. He was wearing jeans and a red T-shirt. Because he was so tanned, it looked really good on him.

Robyn gave me a secretive wink. I was starting to think that coming some place with food was a bad idea, because my stomach was starting to tighten up. I wasn't sure how I was going to eat. I was sitting beside Jake and we were doing something that had absolutely nothing to do with work. I wasn't exactly sure what to say or do.

"Okay, I'm starving, so let's figure out what we're going to eat," Sean said.

We went with an extra large pepperoni and an extra large vegetarian. The guys went to place the order. It was only after they left that I realized I should have gone, too.

"This was my idea," I said. "I should pay."

"Don't worry about it," Caitlin said. "Sean got some money from our parents."

"Yeah, but —"

"Don't worry about it," she insisted again. "You can buy the next round of root beer or something."

"Oh, okay." I was used to being with people who expected me to pay because my dad made so much money. Caitlin and Robyn were just so different from anyone else I'd ever hung around with.

I was sitting next to Robyn. She squeezed

my hand. "Relax. Everything's going to be fine."

"I sorta feel like a fish out of water."

"That's funny," Caitlin said, smiling brightly, "since we're at a water park all day. And now we're not. Get it?"

I rolled my eyes. "I wasn't even thinking about that. I'm having a hard time thinking at all. Major brain freeze going on, and I just don't feel like I'm in charge."

"It's like when we all played miniature golf," Robyn said.

Earlier that summer, I had arranged for some of the people from work to play miniature golf together. "Not really. I could boss people around then. It was my party and I was paying for it." And it had still been a little work-related. Tonight had nothing at all to do with work.

"Didn't Jake hang out with you then?" Robyn asked.

I nodded.

"And he showed up tonight?"

I nodded again.

Robyn grinned. "It has to mean something."

"But *what* exactly?"

Robyn wiggled her eyebrows. "Guess we'll find out."

"What if he tries to kiss me?"

She laughed. "Then it means he likes you."

"And what if he doesn't try to kiss me?"

"Well then, obviously, he's just shy."

I couldn't help myself. I laughed. She was such an optimist. She had a way of making me feel good about myself, of giving me hope that maybe I wasn't crazy to be interested in Jake. "So you think he likes me just because he's here?"

"Absolutely."

I wanted to believe that was true.

The guys came back to the table.

Caitlin started to say something about Paradise Falls, but Sean interrupted her and said we couldn't talk about work. The subject was off-limits. I sort of wanted to know what she was going to say. Learning what people liked and didn't like resulted in improvements and I had no qualms whatsoever about making suggestions.

But Sean was right. It was a lot more interesting talking about other things. I learned that Jake was like me: an only child. He was also like Sean: seventeen. He went to the same public school as everyone at the table except me. It was a large school with more than two thousand students, so they had never met each other before this summer.

Whenever Dad called me on my cell phone — which was usually at least once a day — sometimes we would discuss the advantages and disadvantages of going to a public school. If I went to a public school, I'd attend the same school that my new friends did. And Jake would be there. Not that Dad would see either of those as good reasons to move to a public school. He was all about the studies. But life was more than books. Wasn't that the reason he wanted me to work at the water park? So maybe I would just have to convince Dad to expand his summer project into the fall.

By the time we finished our pizza, I was feeling a lot more comfortable with the group, with Jake, with the test. I thought maybe he was going to pass it. He talked with me. He poured root beer into my mug. He smiled at me a couple of times, like maybe he thought I was interesting.

Then Sean decided that he and Robyn were going to play air hockey. Caitlin looked startled for a moment before announcing that she and Michael were going to play a video game. Which left Jake and me at the table alone. Talk about my friends not being subtle. I had a feeling Robyn had told Sean about the test, but he seemed cool with it.

I was wondering what Jake and I could do. We were too big to play in the little foam balls. I didn't want to go into the bounce house.

"Do you play skee-ball?" Jake asked.

I looked over at the lanes. "It's sorta like bowling, right?"

He laughed. "Yeah, sorta. Come on."

We got up from the table and headed to the skee-ball lanes. Our hands accidentally brushed and I felt this amazing spark of electricity. At least I thought it was an accidental touch. I glanced over at him, and he seemed to be concentrating on something in the distance. The games, I guess, although it looked like he was blushing.

When we got to the alleys, he dropped two quarters into a slot and nine wooden balls rolled out.

"We'll team play," he said. "We'll earn more tickets that way by combining our scores."

"Tickets? You mean like to movies?"

Chuckling, he shook his head. "No. When you earn a certain number of points, you get tickets. Then you take them over to the redemption counter and trade them in for a prize."

"Oh! That sounds like fun." I'd never done anything like this before. Maybe this was part of the real world that my dad wanted to expose me to.

"There are a lot of things you haven't done, aren't there?" he asked.

"Yeah, but I've also done a lot of things. I mean, the possibilities are limitless, so how can anyone do it all?"

"I guess. It's just that it seems like some things you haven't done are normal things that most people do." He shrugged. "That almost sounded like an insult. And that's not what I meant. I guess our worlds are just a little different."

He picked up a ball and rolled it between his hands, as though he was trying to figure it out, or maybe he was feeling awkward about what he'd said. "I'll go first so you can see how it works. You want to roll the ball along the incline and try to get it into one of the holes — the higher the points the more tickets you get."

"Obviously."

"Sorry. I spend too much time talking to kids — explaining ice-cream choices."

There were five holes valued from ten to fifty points. Each hole was smaller than the one before it. In both top corners was a hole valued at a hundred points.

Standing off to the side, I watched as Jake swung his arm back, then forward. He released the ball. It sped up the incline and bounced up to land in the fifty-point hole.

"Oh!" I squealed and clapped. "You're good."

He was grinning broadly. "Probably just lucky. You try."

"Okay." I picked up a ball. It was a lot heavier than I expected. I rolled it between my hands, just like Jake had. I imitated Jake's previous stance, one foot in front of the other. I brought my arm back, swung it forward, released the ball, watched it roll . . . and fall into a trough-looking thing before it ever went up into the area where the holes were.

I looked at Jake. "I'm guessing that I didn't get any points for that."

"You guessed right. You need to roll it a little harder." He picked up a ball, put it in my hand, and stood behind me.

My breath caught. He put his hand beneath mine, so his formed a cocoon around mine.

"Okay, just relax," he ordered.

I nodded, took a breath, and forced myself to relax.

Jake swung my stiff arm back and forth. "Relax, Whitney."

"I *am* relaxed."

"If this is you relaxed, you need to visit a spa or something."

I shook my body, took another deep breath. "Okay."

"Release the ball when I say." He guided my arm back, swung it forward. "Release."

I let go of the ball, it hurtled up the incline and jumped into the target area. It landed off to the side and rolled down into the ten-point area. I released another squeal. "I did it!"

I spun around and would have hugged Jake, but he'd moved back. He slid one hand in the back pocket of his jeans, like he was embarrassed or feeling uncomfortable being around me. He tilted his head forward, indicating the lane. "Try again."

I couldn't deny that I was disappointed that he'd moved away so quickly. It was like he suddenly decided I had cooties or something.

"Okay." I picked up another ball, trying not to feel the sting of rejection. We were just friends out having fun. Nothing more than that.

Maybe it was because I was trying not to think about him, or maybe it was because I was hurt, but I put all my confusion into the swing. The ball raced up the incline, ricocheted off the forty-point target and landed in a hundred.

"Yes!" I did a little dance in a circle, and caught sight of Jake watching me as though he liked me. But maybe he just liked me as a friend. Or maybe Robyn was right — he was just shy. I decided to believe he was shy. It hurt less. It also meant that it was up to me to take charge of the relationship or whatever was going to happen between us.

He went next and earned us another fifty points. We went back and forth after that, taking turns. Mostly I earned ten points. He was good at getting fifty and a hundred. Obviously, he'd played this game a lot.

We ended up spending twenty of his dollars and when we were finished we had sixteen hundred points, which gave us thirty-two tickets. When we got to the prize counter, Jake let me select the prize. My choices were a plastic ring with a lady bug on it or a keychain with purple synthetic fur that I think represented a rabbit's foot.

"Geez, this is really hard," I muttered.

"I've heard lady bugs are lucky," Jake said.

"The ring it is." I handed over the hard-earned tickets and slid the ring onto my pinky. It made me feel a little silly. I'd never worn plastic jewelry before.

We moved away from the counter with two tickets left. Jake handed them to a kid who was on his way to trade his own tickets in.

"Maybe they'll give him what he needs for something awesome," Jake said, grinning.

"I feel so bad," I told him. "You spent twenty dollars and I don't think this ring cost them a dollar."

"It's not about the prize, Whitney. It's about the fun. I had fun playing with you." He was looking at me with those dark brown eyes of his. They made my stomach feel all funny, like butterflies — or maybe lady-bugs — were fluttering inside me.

"I had fun, too."

He studied me for a minute. "So did you come with Robyn or Caitlin?"

"No. Someone dropped me off. I'm supposed to call when I'm ready to go."

"I can take you home. If you want."

Was he kidding? If I *want*? Of course I wanted. Who wouldn't?

"Oh, thanks. Let me call my aunt and let her know."

I moved away from him and took out my cell phone, but I wasn't calling my aunt. I was calling David who was waiting in the limo in the parking lot. I explained that someone else was giving me a ride home.

"That's fine, Miss Whitney, but I'll be watching."

I snapped my phone closed. *Great. Just great.*

Then I looked over to where Jake was standing. He grinned at me.

Yeah, I thought, it *was* great.

CHAPTER FOUR

Jake and I said good-bye to the others. Caitlin winked at me. Robyn grinned. I really hoped that Jake didn't notice. He might wonder what was going on. How would I explain it?

We walked out to the parking lot and to his black truck. I had seen him driving it before. He opened the passenger door and I scrambled up into the seat. I buckled up while he walked around. When he got inside, I said, "I've never ridden in a truck before."

Even with only the parking lot lights filtering in I could see his eyes go round. "You're kidding."

Riding in a truck was probably another one of those things that everyone does that I'd never done.

"Nope," I said. "Dad has a couple of sports cars and a sedan, but no truck. We're really up high."

"Yeah. I like it, because it gives me a good view of everything." He started the engine, shifted into gear, and headed out.

"So what does your dad do?" he asked.

"Oh, you know. Business. How about yours?"

"He's a cop."

"Really?"

He peered over at me really quickly before turning his attention back to the road. "You sound shocked."

"I just never met anyone whose dad was a cop. It's a dangerous job. Do you worry about him?"

"I try not to think about it much, you know?"

"Yeah, I guess so. So what kind of cop is he?"

"What do you mean? Crooked cop?"

I laughed. "No. I mean does he work undercover, cold cases, that sort of thing."

"He worked undercover when he was younger. He'd look so different when he dressed for undercover work that sometimes I didn't recognize him. He'd be all scrungy looking."

"Do you want to be a cop?"

"Maybe. Probably."

I thought about how he always seemed to be looking for trouble, keeping an eye out. I thought he'd make a good police officer.

"What about you?" he asked. "What do you want to do?"

I thought about what would probably happen on Sunday and without planning to, I said, "Survive the summer."

He laughed. "Yeah, I guess we do have to do that, don't we?"

"Most definitely."

We rode in silence for a while. I didn't bother giving Jake directions because he'd been to my house before. It wasn't too difficult to find once someone had been there. It was down a country road, away from the main part of the city. There weren't many houses out where we lived, mostly because each house had been built on several acres of land and each was surrounded by a gated fence with a security monitor. The area was designed for people who really valued their privacy, which made it a little difficult to meet the neighbors. As a matter of fact, I'd never played with anyone in our neighborhood. I didn't even know if any kids my age lived in the immediate area.

Jake took an exit off the expressway. So much for my theory that he remembered the way and knew where he was going.

"You exited too soon," I told him.

"I know. I think someone's following us."

"What?" I twisted around in the seat and looked out the rear window. I could see the limo. Did David *have* to be so obvious? Couldn't he have taken another route home? Or stopped off at a sports bar to catch a baseball game?

Jake suddenly gunned the truck. I released a tiny shriek and jerked around in time to watch him race through a yellow light.

"What are you doing?" I asked.

"If he's following us, he'll go through the red light."

I heard cars honk.

"Shoot! He did." Jake reached into his pocket and pulled out his cell phone.

"Jake —"

"It's okay. The police station is a few blocks over. I'm calling my dad."

This situation was just getting worse. It didn't help that my cell phone started ringing.

"Jake, I know who it is. It's my chauffeur."

He snapped his phone closed, then gave me a hard look that even the shadows couldn't hide. "What?"

"Yeah, I know. Wait a minute." I answered my phone. "Hi, David."

"What's going on, Miss Whitney? Are you all right?"

"I'm fine. We just took the wrong exit."

"Your father wouldn't approve of the lad's reckless driving. He ran through a red light —"

"No, he didn't. The light was still yellow."

"That's not safe driving. Your father wouldn't be pleased."

"We're not going to tell Daddy."

"Not gonna tell Daddy what?" Jake asked, and I heard the panic in his voice.

"Just a minute," I said to Jake, then spoke again to David. "I didn't realize you were going to follow so closely. We're fine. We're getting back on the expressway now. I'll see you at home."

I closed my cell phone and took a deep breath. "I'm sorry about that."

Jake pulled back onto the expressway. "About what exactly? What is going on?"

I wanted to die, right then and there. It was so embarrassing.

"You know I arrive at work in a limo, right?" I asked.

"Yeah, I've seen it. This guy drives you everywhere . . . oh. He's the *someone* who drove you to the Pizza Palace."

I grimaced, even though he couldn't see me squirming in the passenger seat. "Yeah."

"So he was there? You didn't need a ride home?"

I shook my head. He looked at me and I realized he couldn't see me shaking my head. It was harder to say the truth out loud, even though the darkness provided a slight shield. "No, not really."

"Then why didn't you say that at the pizza place?"

Gosh, how was I supposed to answer that? With the truth, no matter how ridiculous or desperate it sounded.

"I like you way more than I like David."

I could see his grin forming in the shadows.

"I'm sorry," I said. "I know taking me home was way out of your way and I had another ride —"

"It's okay."

"Really?"

"Yeah."

He was smiling broadly now. He wasn't mad at all, but I felt so silly. And maybe a little disappointed that he didn't say he liked me, too. Should he have? I just didn't know.

He took the correct exit this time, drove down a ways, and then turned onto the road that would lead us out to the country. I looked in the side-view mirror. David was still following behind us.

"You seem a lot more confident at work," Jake said.

"Can I be honest?"

"Have you been dishonest?"

I groaned. "Well, I didn't tell you about the limo, so I guess I have been, but I was just using a figure of speech."

"Yeah, but it makes you sound like you're not usually honest."

I *was* honest. I just didn't tell people a lot of things. Omission wasn't dishonesty, was it?

"The thing is," I said, not wanting to get into the whole honesty issue, "I'm a little confused about us."

"What do you mean?"

"Can we discuss it when you're not driving?"

"Sure."

We drove in silence while I tried to figure out how to handle this situation, how to explain it exactly. Jake pulled into the drive and stopped by the gate. I gave him the code, and he punched it in. The gates slowly swung open. He drove through and continued down the long drive to the house. He turned onto the circular drive and pulled to a stop in front of the steps leading up to the door. He put the truck in park, then twisted around to face me. His features were illuminated by the lights from the dashboard and those of the limo that pulled to a stop behind us. They were shining on us like a spotlight, like we were two felons who'd escaped from prison.

Thanks, David. Thanks a lot.

"You're confused . . . ?" he asked, prompting me, as though I'd forgotten what we'd been talking about and the answer was a simple fill-in-the-blank.

"Yeah. I mean, we sorta seem to hang out together, but I'm not sure if it means anything."

"Means I like you." He opened his door and got out of the truck before I could think about that or respond.

I was a little stunned. He liked me? But how much did he like me?

I saw him wave at David. Then Jake came around and opened my door. He waited for me to do something. Get out, I guess, but I was still dumbfounded.

"You like me?" I asked.

"Yeah, is that a problem?"

"No, not at all." I grabbed my tote and climbed out of the truck.

We walked to the front door. I turned to him and waited. Was this it? Was this the moment that he kissed me?

Not with David watching. I thought

about calling David on my cell and telling him to go park the limo in the garage.

"See you tomorrow," Jake said.

Before I could say anything, he was hurrying down the steps. I stayed where I was until he was in his truck and driving off. He passed the test with an A-minus. He liked me, but he hadn't kissed me, and even though I understood why he probably hadn't, I couldn't give him points he hadn't earned.

I opened the door and went inside.

"So how was your evening?" Aunt Sophie asked. She was standing in the doorway to the living room. I figured that David had called her and told her we were home. Or maybe she heard the truck arrive.

"It was fun."

"Want to talk about it?"

"Not really." As far as I knew my dad's sister had never had a boyfriend. I didn't think she was the one to go to for advice. "I'm tired and I have work tomorrow."

"Okay. Sweet dreams."

She went back into the living room, and I went upstairs to my bedroom. After I closed my door, I touched the ladybug ring. It was a silly thing: a child's toy, a pretend bit of jewelry. Still, when I took it off, I put it carefully in my jewelry box along with jewelry that cost a good deal more.

Then I changed into my pajamas, climbed into bed, and curled around one of my pillows. Jake said he liked me.

But I still didn't know if he meant he liked me the way you like a friend or a dog or if he meant that he liked me the way you like someone that you want to be with all the time.

CHAPTER FIVE

"So tell us everything that happened," Robyn demanded the next morning when she and Caitlin caught up with me in the locker room.

"Nothing really," I said very casually. I wasn't about to tell them about the car-following-us fiasco that almost resulted in the SWAT team being called out.

"Did he kiss you?" Caitlin asked.

I almost lied and said yes. It was embarrassing to be the only one who hadn't been kissed. Instead, I leaned in close and whispered, "He said he liked me. But no kiss."

And who could blame him with David hovering nearby. I didn't want my first kiss to be in front of an audience — especially an audience who reported to my dad.

"It's coming," Robyn said, like she knew some secret that was about to be revealed. "He's probably just shy."

That seemed to be her explanation for all his behavior that wasn't exactly what I wished it would be. I wasn't so sure that he was shy. I was worried that maybe he just didn't like me *enough* to want to kiss me.

"You might need to give him more hints that you like him," Caitlin said.

"Hints?" I asked. "Like what?"

"Well, according to teen mags, you're supposed to give him little secretive looks and small smiles to encourage him. Find excuses to brush your hand over his. Guys like to feel a hundred percent certain that you're interested, before they kiss you. They don't take rejection well."

"I'm not going to reject him."

"He needs to know that."

"So what? I smile, touch him, and take off my sunglasses so he can see me giving him a secretive look? Not too subtle."

"Yeah, giving the looks is a problem when you work at a water park."

"So just smile at him," Robyn said.

Okay. I could do that. I had a great smile. My braces had come off a year ago, and I invested heavily in teeth-whitening treatments. After staring at a silver smile for two years, I wanted a smile that was as white as I could get it.

With a promise to meet up with them for lunch, I headed over to the offices. Charlotte was leaning against her desk, arms crossed over her chest. Lisa was reading a sheet of paper. "This is going to be a nightmare," Lisa said.

"I prefer to think of it as a challenge," Charlotte replied.

"What's that?" I asked from the doorway.

Lisa looked up and rolled her eyes. "The

luau. The Spencers called this morning with a few" — she made quote marks in the air — "suggestions."

Demands were more like it. Marci wasn't easy to please. I had a feeling that no matter what we did, it wouldn't meet with her approval.

"Why don't we meet back here for another brainstorming session after the last birthday party today?" Charlotte suggested.

We'd met briefly yesterday afternoon. So far, we had decided to have leis. I liked Charlotte a lot, but she didn't have much imagination. It seemed someone in her position, who was in charge of "entertainment," should at least have a vivid, if not a wild, imagination.

"All right," Lisa said. She sighed. "We've got six parties this morning and four this afternoon so we'd better get to it."

"Why so many?" I asked. It wasn't unusual to have that many on the weekend, but not on a weekday.

"Who knows? Full moon, I guess," Lisa said. "All the little monsters come out to play."

With clipboard in hand, she led the way outside. We nearly ran into Jake, who was pushing the stainless steel ice-cream cart in the direction of Mini Falls.

"We're gonna need extra ice cream today," Lisa said, without breaking her stride.

"Got it!" Jake called out to her. "Saw the message you left on my locker and the one you left on the cart."

I don't know if Lisa heard him. She was power walking to the pavilion, leaving us behind. Of course it didn't take much for her to power walk. She was almost six feet tall, so she had long legs that covered a lot of ground fast. I was all of five feet four. My legs couldn't keep up with her. Or maybe I was staying behind on purpose so I could talk to Jake.

"She's control-freak central," Jake muttered.

"But she gets the job done."

He glanced over at me. "You know, when I filled out my application to work here, I thought I'd be a big, bad lifeguard. Not the scoop guy. It's such a wimpy job."

"It's an important job," I assured him. Plus, it kept him working near me. If he was a lifeguard, I'd probably never see him. I might not have ever even met him. We wouldn't have gotten to know each other.

"Don't you want to be a lifeguard?" he asked, almost like where I worked influenced where he worked. "Maybe we could work at the same pool."

Paradise Falls had several pools, each offering its own unique setting. I was encouraged that he wanted us to work in the same area, but I wasn't really into the pools, especially after the near-drowning earlier in the summer. Being a lifeguard was a lot of responsibility.

"I like working in parties because things change every day. At the pools, it just all stays the same," I said.

"The scenery changes."

Scenery was guy-talk for girls. I knew this because it was also Caitlin's code for guys. Before she'd started dating Michael, she was all about the "scenery" at Tsunami.

"Besides, parties are pretty much the same for me," Jake said. "Scoop, dip, scoop, dip. You have any idea how cold my hands get?"

"Oh, poor thing. Do you know how *hot* it gets standing around watching kids play?"

"But how hard is it?"

"Like I said, boring."

"I guess no one is ever really happy with their jobs."

"I am," I said. "Ever since I moved to parties."

We arrived at the pavilion.

"Come on, y'all!" Lisa called out to us. "We need balloons! We need setup! Make yourself useful, Whitney. I can't do everything."

"I thought she liked doing everything," I muttered.

"Don't take it personally," Jake said as he headed over to the helium canister.

"I wasn't taking it personally." Okay, maybe I was a little. She'd never gotten after me before. Maybe she was feeling stressed with the big luau coming up. We only had four days to prepare for it. Theoretically, I guess we didn't have to do anything other than have the park open to the party guests, but we had a reputation to maintain so we did what we could to provide something extra.

A storage shed was off to the side, cleverly disguised to look like a straw hut. I went inside, grabbed six sand pails, and filled them with all kinds of cheap trinkets. I put a pail on each table that had been designated for a party. Lisa had already put the reservation sign with the party's name on it on each table. Jake was fast with the balloons. He had half the tables ready to go.

The bells sounded, signaling the opening of the park.

"Whitney, get to the front gate!"

"Geez, don't get your shorts in a knot," I mumbled as I hurried to the front of the park.

The gates that the customers used followed a long path past the parrot and came to an end near Tsunami. To one side was Tsunami, and beyond that Thrill Hill, which was where most of the rides and amusements were. The other side led through the shops, the food court, and on to Mini Falls, which was the kiddie zone. Since most birthday parties were for kids younger than twelve, we used the pavilions in Mini Falls so parents didn't have to watch their kids quite so closely. Even so, Mini Falls was where Robyn and I had rescued the little boy who had nearly drowned. So although the water at Mini Falls was the shallowest in the park, we had more lifeguards per number of guests there than in any other area of the park.

I held up a sign with the names of each birthday party on it. When someone from the group, usually a parent, approached me, I gave her or him a map and explained how to get to the pavilion where the party was being arranged. If we were doing only a couple of parties, we'd escort them, but six was just too many to handle in that manner. And people who arrived on time didn't like waiting around for those who didn't. Once I had everyone on the list marked off, I headed back to the party pavilion.

It was chaos when I got there. They'd brought Robyn over to help. Sometimes they did that — recruited some of the lifeguards or ride attendants in the area to keep an eye on things or help us out.

"Mad Mother warning," she said as I neared.

"Reminds me of mad cow disease," I told her.

"That would probably be better. She doesn't like the location of her table."

"You're kidding?"

"No, the table is at the back, and she thinks that makes it seem like her child isn't very important."

"The tables are assigned in the order of when people call in to make their reservations." The big board in the office had all the tables on the grid, and we started at one side, filling in the grids as reservations came in — no favorites. It was simply first called in, first served.

"I think Lisa's trying to explain that to her," Robyn said.

I looked past Robyn. A woman with a face so red that it almost matched her hair was yelling at Lisa. Yelling about a stupid table. She was acting the way Marci did when she didn't get her way. It made me angry that people could be unreasonable.

I walked over. Lisa must have seen me out of the corner of her eye because she held up her hand like a cop directing traffic at a concert.

"This is just outrageous," the woman said. "I paid good money for this party and we can't even see the water because all these other people are in front of us."

"Ma'am, I'm really sorry," Lisa said.

"You shouldn't be," I said. Both Lisa and the woman looked at me. Well, Lisa looked, the woman glared. I was wishing I'd kept my mouth shut but the park didn't pay the employees enough for them to get yelled out. "All these other people made their reservations first. You snooze, you lose."

Lisa took in a sharp breath. The woman looked like a balloon with too much air in it that was about to burst.

"I'm sure we can make this right," Lisa said.

"There's nothing to make right," I said.

"Whitney," Lisa growled. "I'll handle this."

"But you shouldn't have —"

"Whitney, no matter what you say or do, you're not going to get in trouble for it. I will. So just go away." She made little fluttering motions with her hands, like she was trying to sweep me away.

"Lisa —"

"Go away. Right now. That's an order."

I started to say something else, and she shushed me. That stung. I wasn't used to getting shushed.

I spun on my heel and walked across the

pavilion. Robyn caught up with me. I must have had a determined expression on my face, because she grabbed my arm. "Where are you going?"

"I don't know."

"You can't just leave."

"Wanna bet?"

I thought about calling David, telling him to come back to get me. I thought about going into the general manager's office and announcing, "I quit!"

Only I didn't want to quit. If the idea of Marci coming here wasn't enough to make me quit, some witchy woman certainly wasn't going to do it.

Walking around the perimeter of the park, I watched people floating in the river that circled the park. More people would be there later in the day. They always hit the rides first, then relaxed in the afternoon. I was tempted to jump into the river — park uniform and all.

Instead I kept walking.

Maybe getting yelled at was the real world that Dad had wanted me exposed to. I didn't understand people yelling to try to get what they wanted. I always got what I wanted and I didn't yell to do it. I just asked for it like I expected to get it.

It was all in the attitude.

Of course, Lisa had pretty much shot my attitude down. And what did she mean by saying that I wouldn't get in trouble but she would? Because she was the supervisor? Or did she know the truth about my dad?

I finally made it around to Tsunami. If I walked a little farther, I'd hit the offices where I could go and complain. That was my plan: to tell them that I didn't like Lisa's attitude, but when I spotted Caitlin stretched out on a lounge chair, I decided I'd rather talk to her.

I walked over and asked. "Why aren't you working?"

Caitlin slipped her sunglasses on before opening her eyes to look at me. "I'm on break. What are you doing here?"

"I was ordered to go away." I sat on the lounge chair beside hers.

"Why?" she asked.

I shrugged. "Some mother wasn't happy with her party table. I tried to calm her down, and Lisa told me to go away, like it wasn't my problem."

"Well, she is the supervisor, so technically it's her job to take care of problems."

"Still, the mother was unreasonable. I was just trying to point that out."

Caitlin shook her head. "I don't understand people."

"Me either."

"So what — now you're just wandering around?"

"Pretty much."

"Must be nice."

I heard something in her voice that sounded a little catty. "What's that supposed to mean?"

"It's not like you really *work* here."

"Of course I *work* here."

"Not really. You get to do whatever you want. The rest of us have to do what we're told."

I felt so unappreciated. Parties and Entertainment might not be in charge of saving lives, but we were important. We helped to bring people to the park. "I'm doing what I was told. I went away."

"She probably didn't mean far away and forever. She probably just meant away from her."

I sighed, shrugged. "Then she should have said precisely what she meant."

And I was not going to feel guilty that they had six birthday parties and a bunch of kids to deal with — without me around. They would just have to find someone else. Maybe then they would appreciate me a little more. I figured they'd need at least two people to replace me. I was that good at handling parties. I made sure people felt important.

Caitlin rolled to a sitting position. "Don't you ever worry about getting fired?"

"No."

"Well, I do, so I better get back to my station."

I watched her walk over the sand-covered deck to the lifeguard tower where she'd watch all the swimmers. I couldn't imagine anything more boring that sitting around watching other people having fun. At least with the parties, I was involved. I talked with people, helped them solve problems — like when they were a party favor short or dropped their cake on the way in — took their pictures so they'd have the memories. I got to move around, dance when they brought music, sing when they didn't. I liked what I did. It was almost like I was in charge, except when Lisa told me to go away.

It wasn't fair that the woman was upset with Lisa, and it wasn't fair that Lisa got upset with me. We could have offered the woman free tickets so she could come to the park another day. People usually forgave anything for free tickets. That was what I had wanted to say.

Real world indeed.

I didn't much like it. I closed my eyes and tried not to think about what had happened at the pavilion. An image of Marci with her professionally straightened auburn hair filled my mind. I didn't want to think about her either. I wanted to think about something interesting, which led me to thinking about Jake. I wondered if he would have kissed me if David hadn't been around. Should I have kissed him?

I didn't even know how to go about it. Oh, I knew the basics, but I didn't know how to initiate it. Maybe he didn't either. Weren't we a great pair?

Some time later I heard squeaking wheels rolling in the distance. They reminded me of the ice-cream cart that Jake pushed around. Scooping ice cream probably was the most boring job, although it did have one perk. It gave him a chance to work with me.

"Brooding?"

I opened one eye. Jake was standing there. His question didn't deserve an answer. I looked at my watch. "Are the parties over already?"

"Yep. I'm off to refill the ice-cream carts for round two of insanity."

When we didn't have any parties going on, Jake set up his cart in Mini Falls and sold ice cream. It was where we'd first met. He'd been selling ice cream near Splash where Robyn and I had worked. Come to think of it, he didn't become the permanent ice-cream party guy until I moved to P&E. I wondered if he requested the transfer. Something to think about.

"So did the woman ever stop yelling?" I asked.

"Yeah. Lisa gave her complimentary park tickets."

"That's what I was going to suggest before I was told to disappear."

"She didn't actually tell you to disappear. She just said she'd handle it."

"Whatever. Are you on her side?"

"There are no sides here." He sighed. "I didn't really come over here to talk about work."

"Why *did* you come over here?"

He rocked on his heels, adjusted his red visor. "I don't know." He started to walk away, stopped, and looked back at me. "You like baseball?"

Where did that question come from? "You mean to watch it or to play it?"

I could see his brow wrinkling. "What difference does it make?"

"Well, if it's to play it, not really." I wasn't going to admit I'd never played, plus with sports, the players usually got sweaty. I really wasn't into getting sweaty. Within the water park, outdoor fans and mist-makers kept things reasonably comfortable, and I had opportunities to go into the offices. "If it's to watch it, maybe."

"Maybe?"

"I've seen a couple of games on TV, but I've never actually gone to a game."

His mouth dropped open. "You're kidding?"

"Nope."

"Huh." He shook his head. "Tomorrow's your day off, right?"

"Yeah."

"My dad and I were going to a game tomorrow night, but he has to work. So I have an extra ticket. Want to go?"

Did that make it a hand-me-down ticket? I wasn't really into hand-me-downs, second-chance stores, garage sales, or used items. They all had an ickiness factor. I mean, if someone else didn't want them, why would I?

On the other hand, the ticket hadn't been used *and* it was a chance to do something with Jake. It was almost a date. Almost. It wasn't like he'd planned to ask me. I was his fallback option since his dad couldn't go. But it was better than not being an option at all.

"Yeah, I do want to go," I said. "Thanks."

"Great. Game starts at seven. I'll pick you up at six."

"Okay."

"And see if you can get the limo guy not to follow."

I laughed. "Not a problem."

Or at least I didn't think it would be. I needed to get Aunt Sophie's permission to go out with Jake at all.

And *that* could be a problem.

CHAPTER SIX

"Just you and this boy?" Aunt Sophie asked, like the words didn't fit together into a sentence she could decipher.

We were sitting at the counter in the kitchen. It was Wicked Wednesday, the day when Aunt Sophie ordered in pizza. Even though she was slender, she had high cholesterol, so she ate healthy six days a week. But she believed everyone was entitled to a bad day now and then.

"Yeah, I mean it's kinda sort of a date, but not really a date. I mean, it's a *baseball game*." I made it sound like it was something worse than wearing designer knockoffs. Maybe if she thought I didn't desperately want this, she'd be okay with it.

"And what's his name?"

"Jake. Remember? You knew who he was last night." How could she forget in less than twenty-four hours?

"Oh, right. And he wants to pick you up and drive you?"

"Yeah."

She bit into the pizza loaded with everything and sighed happily. She chewed, swallowed, and pursed her lips. "Bad things happen at baseball parks, Whitney. They have dangerous stuff there. Hot dogs, nachos, cotton candy —"

Oh, yeah, the dangers were everywhere. She obviously hadn't looked over the menu at Scavenger's, a little restaurant at the water park. "I'll eat before I go."

"Is anyone else going?" she asked.

I groaned. "I don't know. Maybe ten thousand fans."

She narrowed her eyes at me. "I meant with you and Jake. I know group dating is popular with kids your age. I'm trying to determine exactly what the situation is here."

"Aunt Sophie, I work with Jake every day. He's a nice guy. And I'm not sure it's really a date. Like I said, he had this extra ticket and invited me. We're just buddies."

She sighed. "All right. You can go —"

"Yes!"

"— but there are restrictions. You need to be home by ten thirty and I want you to use your cell phone to send me a picture of the scoreboard at the top of each inning."

"Why would you care about the score?"

"I don't. But that way I know you're at the game."

"If you don't trust me you shouldn't let me go," I grumbled, realizing that I could be convincing her to change her mind about letting me go. On the other hand, it was sort of a reverse psychology thing, making her prove she trusted me instead of me proving I could be trusted. All the money Dad had spent on Dr. Succop wasn't totally wasted.

Aunt Sophie reached over and tugged on

my hair. "All right. No pics. But do be home by ten thirty."

I got up, wrapped my arms around her, and hugged her tightly. "Thanks, Aunt Sophie."

"If you really want to thank me, bring me back a bag of cotton candy."

"Isn't that bad for your triglycerides?"

"Only if *I* buy it."

I laughed. Aunt Sophie never seemed to mind taking care of me. She had her own place in town, but when Dad was away on business, she stayed here. She illustrated children's books, so she could pretty much work anywhere she wanted. I still looked through the books that she'd illustrated. I liked her drawings.

I sat back down to finish eating my pizza. It seemed a lonely life for her. Maybe I *would* bring her some cotton candy. Seemed like the least I could do.

"I knew you couldn't *not* buy anything," Caitlin said.

It was the next day, our day off. Caitlin, Robyn, and I were at a shoe store in the mall. Caitlin was looking at her reflection in the mirror, twisting one foot then the other, admiring the gold leather thong sandals that I was going to have to buy for her, because I lost our bet. Within half an hour of our arrival at the mall, I purchased a pair of aqua Capris and the cutest top. I'd come to the shoe store to find matching sandals.

"Well, I've got my first official date tonight." Date. That sounded so strange to say. And even though I was the backup plan for Jake, I'd decided to treat it like it was the original plan and was a real date. Who knew? Maybe it would be. "I couldn't *not* buy something new to wear. A true friend would have postponed the bet."

She scoffed. "Yeah, well, there is friend-ship and then there are shoes, and shoes always win. I can't believe I'm wearing Jimmy Choos."

"They look really good," I told her.

"Yeah, I know."

With a sigh, Caitlin sat down, and the clerk carefully removed the sandals from her feet.

"Shall I wrap these up?" he asked.

"Nah, I just wanted to try them on. But thanks."

"You're not getting them?" I asked.

"No." She slipped back on her own shoes — sandals with little cheap rhinestones along the straps. "I'm not going to have you spend four hundred and fifty dollars for a pair of shoes."

"My dad will be the one doing the spending and he won't even notice. A bet is a bet."

"Yeah, well . . ." She stood up and slung her tote bag over her shoulder. "Like I'm really going to make you buy me shoes. Get real."

She headed out of the store. Unsure what to do, I looked at Robyn. "We had a bet."

She shrugged. "She's always wanted to come here. She figured they wouldn't chase her out if she came with someone who probably *does* buy her shoes here. Don't worry.

She's been eyeing some purple flip-flops with silver sparkles on them. You can get those for her."

"She's all about the sparkles, isn't she?"

"And the friendship."

It was so strange. I'd never had friends who didn't want something from me. I might not have realized it at the time, but it always came down to what I could give them. Robyn and Caitlin were different. So very different.

I bought the sandals that I'd selected, apologized to the guy for putting him through all that trouble with Caitlin for nothing, took his business card, and promised to ask for him when I came back to shop for shoes for school. I would bring Aunt Sophie, too. He would earn enough commission from her shoe sales to put him through a semester at college.

I left the store and saw Robyn and Caitlin standing together, looking over the second-floor railing, down onto the concourse below. They were so comfortable with each other. I wanted that kind of friendship. I didn't know how to get it.

"So, what now?" I asked.

They both turned to face me.

"Cheesecake Factory?" Caitlin suggested.

"Works for me."

To my surprise, we didn't have to wait, maybe because it was a weekday. We were taken to a booth and placed our orders. It seemed I wasn't the only one who had memorized the menu on previous visits. Caitlin and Robyn didn't even open their menus.

"Okay," Robyn said, leaning forward on her elbows. "Everyone's talking about the luau, so give us the scoop."

"What do you mean everyone's talking about it? It's only been a couple of days since we got the party order."

"What can I say? The secret is out. So spill it."

It was a little unsettling to know that gossip and news traveled so fast around the park. Not that the party was a secret. And Charlotte and Lisa were really worried about it, so there was no telling who they'd told. The park was sometimes rented after hours to companies. They didn't expect much. Just lifeguards to be on duty and the concession stands to be open. But people paying for a birthday party expected more. And the Spencers expected us to pull out all the stops. They wanted a party their daughter would never forget. After all, she didn't turn sixteen every day.

"Well, Charlotte is her usual unimaginative self. She suggested leis again." We met yesterday afternoon for further brainstorming. "Lisa's great at making things happen. You just have to tell her what you want to happen."

"But you, my friend," Caitlin said, pointing at me, "are the party genius."

I felt myself blushing at her calling me her friend, even as I tried to act cool by pointing at myself. "I am. I suggested that we really give Tsunami an island atmosphere. My big idea was a bonfire in the sand near the water."

While Marci wasn't my friend anymore, I was feeling a little protective and competitive about Paradise Falls. I wanted us to put on an event that everyone who attended — and maybe even everyone who worked there — would be talking about for summers to come.

"Isn't that dangerous?" Robyn asked.

"Not if we move everything back so nothing is around to catch on fire — except for the wood of the bonfire, of course. And we won't make it huge or anything. People do it on beaches all the time. Plus I thought we could have a clambake, limbo dancing — that's where you have a pole that people try to go under without knocking it off its stand. The pole just gets lower and lower and lower. Then I thought we could hire a live band."

"Sounds like a blast. *I* want to go to this party," Caitlin said.

"You probably will, because we'll need all the lifeguards."

"Yeah, but sitting in the tower watching people isn't as much fun as being down there partying with them. Maybe we could have an employee party right after and use all the great things you've got planned for this one."

"My plans haven't been approved yet."

"But they will be. When has the park ever said no to you?"

"I don't know —"

"You made it happen for the employees before."

I had. Earlier in the summer, I arranged an employee get-together night. But it had cost the park very little — just some hot dogs and a few other refreshments. What we were planning for the luau would be costly.

"I'll see," I said, not making a total commitment.

"I think it would be so romantic," Robyn said. "I've never been on a tropical island."

Of course, I had. Dad and I had taken cruises, flown to islands on his private jet for long weekends. Yes, we were wealthy. The funny thing was that how much money my family had didn't seem important to Robyn or Caitlin.

Caitlin put her elbow on the table, her chin in her palm. "Who are you, Whitney St. Clair — and why do you have so much power?"

I almost told them, almost told them everything. But I liked being a little mysterious. So I laughed instead. "If I had power, Lisa wouldn't have told me to go away yesterday."

"That ballistic mother was so weird," Robyn said.

"Actually, she was a preview for what we might have to deal with when the Spencers' party takes place," I said.

"You think they'll be that bad?" Robyn asked.

"Count on it."

When we finished eating, we walked around the mall a little longer, trying on different outfits, laughing at one another, challenging each other to get outrageous with clothing choices, but not buying anything. All of it was a strange experience for me. I usually shopped with Aunt Sophie.

Well, that wasn't exactly true. I *bought* with Aunt Sophie. She wasn't much of a shopper, but she was a real buyer. She went to stores to buy things, not to shop around. She always knew what she wanted, went in, and bought it. She didn't goof around.

I discovered that I liked goofing around. Hanging out with Robyn and Caitlin was way more fun than hanging out with Aunt Sophie. I felt a little guilty thinking that, because I liked Aunt Sophie. But she was my aunt, not my girlfriend. It was strange to think that I might have BFFs again.

Since I needed plenty of time to get ready for my *date*, we left the mall late in the afternoon. We were all fifteen; none of us had driver's licenses, so I provided the transportation. David gave Robyn and Caitlin a ride home. He dropped Robyn off first, then we went to Caitlin's house. She lived only a couple of streets over. She could have walked from Robyn's, but David was all about service and taking care of his passengers.

When David pulled to a stop in front of Caitlin's house, she said, "Wait here just a sec."

David left the back door open while Caitlin hurried into the house. I couldn't imagine what I needed to wait for. It was a couple of minutes before she came rushing back out. She stepped into the limo and sat on the plush leather seat beside me.

"Here. It's one of my favorites."

She handed me a necklace with unevenly-shaped aqua stones in a circle. One teardrop stone hung downward and was caught in a silver oval.

"It'll look great with your new outfit," she said.

I stared at her. I didn't know what to say.

"Are you giving this to me?" I asked, dumbfounded.

"I'm letting you borrow it. I got it when we went on vacation in New Mexico last year. I bought it from an artist at a little sidewalk stand. It's one of a kind. Trust me. You'll look hot."

Caitlin and I had always had this sort of love-hate relationship going. I really didn't know what to make of her gesture. It was taking our relationship to another level, one I'd never experienced. "I've never borrowed anything." If I needed it, I bought it.

"Well, now you have. That's what friends do. Swap things." She got out of the car and then looked back in, wiggled her eyebrows. "Text us if he kisses you."

Then she was gone.

Text them? I leaned back and smiled. I'd call them.

Caitlin was right. The necklace was perfect.

I wasn't. My hair didn't want to settle into place properly. The mascara kept leaving behind little black dots because I blinked before my eyelashes were dry. And Aunt Sophie, almost as nervous as I was about the date, came in to check on me, caught me using her makeup, and ordered me to wash it all off.

"But Aunt Sophie — "

"No arguments. You look like a Cirque du Soleil performer."

I hated to admit that she was right. I *had* applied it a little heavily. But then, this was my first real date. I wanted to be beautiful. I wanted Jake not to take his eyes off me. If he still thought of me as a buddy, I wanted him to think of me as something more.

Aunt Sophie stood like a prison warden, arms crossed over her chest, making sure I did what she'd ordered. After I finished drying my face, she said, "Sit down."

I looked at her. She pointed to the small bench in front of my vanity. I did as she ordered. She came over and started messing with my face, applying a little rouge and mascara.

"These aren't really the right shades for you," she said. "Wait another year, when you're just a little bit older, and we'll go makeup shopping."

She was brushing powder over my face. "Do not tell your dad that I let you walk out of the house in makeup." She leaned back and smiled. "What do you think?"

I looked in the mirror. It didn't look like I was wearing makeup, and yet it did. "Perfect."

She was standing with me in the foyer when Jake's big black truck rumbled into the drive. With a small leather tote over my shoulder, I headed outside. Aunt Sophie followed. She gave Jake all kinds of rules: home by ten thirty, no crazy driving, and no bad behavior that might cause my dad to get out his shotgun.

"My dad doesn't have a shotgun," I mumbled later as I buckled up after Jake got back behind the wheel.

Jake grinned. "That's good to hear."

His teasing made me wonder if he was planning on some bad behavior. Did I want him thinking about behaving badly? I was pretty sure that I didn't.

Jake was wearing a baseball cap, a maroon T-shirt, and jeans. I didn't think he'd gone to nearly as much trouble as I had to get ready. I felt a little silly, maybe even a little overdressed. This was a date, right? Or were we just friends hanging out?

Had he asked me out because he felt sorry for me? Because Lisa had yelled at me? I just didn't know what to think. I was back to being unable to accurately define our relationship.

On the way to the baseball field, we talked about the water park and the insanity of the birthday parties. I told him about some of the plans for the luau.

"Your friend will be impressed that you've thought of all these things to make her birthday special," he said.

I scoffed. "Yeah, right. Besides, I don't plan to let her know I was involved."

"Why not?"

"I just don't want her to know I'm there."

I guess he heard in my voice that I didn't want to talk about it. I'd made up my mind.

I could do everything behind the scenes, never be discovered . . . or uncovered. My secrets would remain safe.

And as long as my secrets were kept, I wasn't in danger of losing the new friends I'd made this summer.

Jake and I arrived at the baseball field. It was a long walk from the parking lot to the gate. I was disappointed that we didn't hold hands. I considered being bold and taking his hand. That would certainly make a statement about my feelings for him, but I was a chicken. What if I took his hand and he looked at me like I was crazy? Did guys like boldness in a girl? Or did they want to make all the moves? Should I text Robyn for some advice?

Jake gave our tickets to the gate attendant, who scanned them. Then we walked through the gate. We started working our way through the crowd of people.

Jake reached back and took my hand. His hand was large, mine so small. I wanted to think it meant something special that we were holding hands, but I suspected it was just that he didn't want us to get separated. He seemed to know where he was going.

I'd been here once, earlier in the summer, for a fireworks show. Sean had invited me that time. We sat on a quilt on the grassy knoll. I was really hoping that Jake's tickets were for real seats.

We stopped at the concession stand and bought hot dogs and drinks. Then we walked to a section behind home plate. "Follow me," Jake said, and he started down the steps.

Thank goodness. No grassy knoll. I wasn't a huge fan of bugs. Jake kept on going down the steps until he was five rows from the bottom. We were on the aisle. I took the inside seat.

"These are great seats," I said.

"Yeah. My dad buys season tickets. We don't make it to all the games, but we always have great seats when we do."

I bit into my hot dog. "Oh, this is good."

"Ballpark hot dogs are the best. I don't know why, but they're always better than you'll get anywhere else."

"The ones at Paradise Falls are good," I said, feeling a need to defend the park and its offerings.

He grinned. "I don't think they're this good."

I smiled back at him. "Almost."

I finished eating my hot dog as people began filling in the seats around us. When the game started and the first player went up to the plate, I took out my cell phone.

"What are you doing?" Jake asked.

"Sending my aunt proof that we're at the game." I thought a player at bat was more interesting than the scoreboard. I snapped the picture and sent it to her.

"She needed proof?" he asked.

I peered over at him and shrugged. "What can I say? You heard her spouting off the rules."

"Your dad is pretty protective, isn't he?"

"Afraid so. But it's just because I'm his princess. His words, not mine. He gets back from his business trip tomorrow. You'll have to meet him."

Jake shifted in his seat as though he was suddenly really uncomfortable. He turned his attention back to the game.

I was such an idiot. No matter how much I loved my dad, guys didn't want to meet fathers. Plus I was assuming a lot — like maybe Jake would ask me out again, that I wasn't just a seat-filler. That there was a reason for him to meet my dad, like maybe we'd do more things together.

"So which team are we rooting for?" I wanted to change the subject and get things comfortable between us again.

Jake grinned at me. He really had the cutest grin. "The home team, of course. Rough Riders. I can't believe you've never been to a baseball game."

"My dad likes football."

"I like football, too. It's not like you can have only one sport."

"But he's busy with business."

I thought I saw sympathy in Jake's expression.

"But that's okay," I told him, "because it makes tonight really special. You'll always be the guy who took me to my first baseball game."

My words sounded so pathetic, as though I was trying to force Jake to be special, or force him to see me as special. Why couldn't I just enjoy the game and stop worrying about what being here said about us?

The pitcher struck out the first three batters. Our team was up to bat. I was sneaking a peek at Jake when I heard a crack. The player had hit the ball hard, right out of the park. Jake came to his feet and punched his arm in the air. "Yeah!"

He looked down at me. "You do know what a home run is, don't you?"

"Of course. I've *seen* baseball — like in the movies and stuff."

"Then come on! Get into it."

I stood up, and even though I felt silly, I punched the air, too. "Yeah!"

Jake leaned down and brushed his shoulder against mine. "That's more like it."

I smiled at him. He was so much fun.

The announcer announced that they'd be passing around a boot, taking donations that would go to the player's favorite charity. Jake and I each put a dollar in the boot when it made it down our row.

I tried to pay attention to the game, but I was more interested in the various activities happening around the edge of the field. The mascot was someone dressed up like a gigantic prairie dog. His antics were hilarious. The games they played in between innings had me thinking about how we could adapt them to use at parties held at Paradise Falls.

Then in the sixth inning, they displayed a heart on the video screen, and the camera zoomed in on a couple who would then kiss. Someone with a camera was walking around close to where Jake and I were sitting. I held my breath, wondering what we'd do if the camera focused on us. Would it be a real kiss? Did I want hundreds of people I didn't know to witness my very first kiss?

Jake picked up his program and started reading player stats. I wondered if he was nervous, too, if he was trying to figure out what we would do.

The camera zoomed in on two guys in the visitors' dugout. They waved the camera away, but it stayed on them. One guy leaned over and pretended to kiss the other one. The crowd laughed and clapped. Then the kiss cam went off the video screen, and the umpire called out, "Play ball."

"That was kinda crazy," I said.

"Yeah. It can get even crazier, though. They don't always realize who's together. Once they put the camera on my dad and the woman sitting beside him. Unfortunately, she wasn't my mom. She was someone we didn't even know."

"What did your dad do?"

Jake shrugged. "What could he do? They wouldn't move the camera on, so he kissed her on the cheek."

So Jake *would* have kissed me. Question was: Would it have been because he wanted to or because he felt like he had no choice?

The game was over by nine thirty. Our team won, one to nothing. The only score came from that home run. Before the game was over, I bought a bag of cotton candy to take to Aunt Sophie.

By the time we got to the parking lot, it was a little after ten. We didn't talk much on the drive home. The closer we got to my house, the more nervous I became. I opened the bag and snitched a little cotton candy so my mouth would be sweet — just in case. I thought that was better than scrounging around in my tote for a cinnamon breath strip.

Jake pulled to a stop outside the front porch. We opened our doors at the same time, climbed out, and met near the front of

129

the truck. Jake looked at the door. I looked at him. He stuck his hands in his back pockets. "Well, thanks for going with me," he said.

"Anytime your dad can't go . . ." Did I really say that? Had I just invited myself along? Aunt Sophie would be horrified by my boldness.

Jake took a step back. "I'll just stand here and make sure you get in all right." Was that guy-talk for no kiss?

"It's not like I'm going to get mugged," I said.

"Still, it's the way my dad taught me."

His dad, the cop, had taught him to watch out for people.

"Well, then, okay." I felt awkward and silly. I thought about just stepping over and kissing *him*. But did I really want my first kiss to be one that I gave a guy — a guy who didn't seem to be too interested in kissing me? "Thanks. I had fun."

"See you at work tomorrow."

I nodded. "Okay."

Disappointed, I walked up the steps and opened the door. I looked back over my shoulder and waved at Jake. Then I went inside. I heard a truck door slam, heard the roar of the engine as the truck started, and heard the rumble of the tires over the pebbled drive as Jake drove away.

I had no reason to be sad. The night had been fun. Not all guys kissed on the first date. Jake was probably shy — just like Robyn kept telling me. He said he liked me. Tonight there had been no spotlight on us. So why didn't he kiss me?

Maybe Aunt Sophie could shed some light on the things that were confusing me. Besides, I needed to give her the cotton candy.

I looked in the living room. Aunt Sophie wasn't there. I could see light coming from the direction of the kitchen. I headed that way and stumbled to a stop in the doorway.

Aunt Sophie was in the kitchen, sitting at the counter. So was David. They were holding hands and smiling at each other.

Romance was going on right under my nose. How had that happened and how had I missed it?

CHAPTER SEVEN ୨

"Your aunt and the chauffeur?" Robyn asked the next morning, clearly as mystified as I had been last night when I'd spied the lovebirds.

We were standing near Tsunami before we all headed off in different directions to get to our assigned positions. Caitlin and Robyn had cornered me, wanting to know the scoop about my date with Jake, but sadly it wasn't nearly as interesting as what I'd discovered in the kitchen. "My aunt and the chauffeur," I repeated.

"Wasn't that a Disney movie?" Caitlin asked.

"I don't think so."

"How could they like each other and you not know?" Robyn asked.

"You've been to my house. We can go days without seeing each other. So I guess they were hanging around together and I never saw them. If I hadn't gotten home a little early last night, I might not have ever seen them. I'm just a little freaked out."

"I think it's great," Robyn said.

"But what if they get married? Who'll take care of me when Dad is out of town?"

Robyn gave me a warm smile. "You can stay with me."

"Really?"

"Sure. It's just Mom and me. She won't mind. So let's get back to Jake. How was your date?"

I still hadn't decided and I wasn't sure how much I wanted to reveal. Would I look like a total loser if I confessed that he hadn't kissed me? *When in doubt, stall.* I glanced at my watch. "No time. I'll tell you all about it during lunch."

I headed to the office. Fridays were always killers. The only worse day was Saturday. Sunday wasn't as bad, but still it was no picnic — well, unless you were celebrating a birthday. Then a picnic was usually involved.

I walked into the office building. The receptionist looked up. "Uh, Mr. T wants to see *you*?"

Her voice rose at the end, making the statement sound like she was questioning whether I was the person he wanted to see. How strange. It was as though she was afraid of me or something. "Okay."

I strolled down the hallway to his office. His last name was difficult to pronounce, so he just went by Mr. T. Even the sign beside his door just read, MR. T.

The door was open. Still, I knocked on the doorjamb. He looked up from something he was studying and smiled at me. "Whitney, come on in. Have a seat."

I sat in the leather chair in front of his desk. Mr. T had fading red hair. He was slender and in good shape. I'd seen him hop onto benches when he wanted to be seen so he could address a crowd of people. I liked him.

"How are you doing?" he asked.

"Doing good."

"Good. Good. Good."

Okay, there were too many goods being bandied about. I had a theory that when someone kept saying good, it was because something was bad.

"Is everything okay?" I asked.

He steepled his fingers and tapped them together. "I'm glad you asked, because I have a bit of a problem."

I wasn't at all surprised to hear that. I was a little surprised that he was telling me, but I decided that maybe he saw me as a problem solver — a creative thinker.

"I'm short an employee in the Treasure Chest gift shop. I'd like you to fill in. I know you don't have any cash register experience so you'd just take care of, uh, you know — answering questions and helping customers."

136

"You mean, like a sales associate?"

"More like a helper."

"But what about parties? On Friday we're usually swamped."

He cleared his throat. "Well, when you were AWOL the other morning, Lisa found a couple of people to help her. They helped yesterday, too, so we moved them into parties."

"Oh. But I wasn't really AWOL. She told me to leave."

"I think she meant for you to leave the situation alone, not to leave the area."

"But —"

"Whitney, I need you to work in the gift shop."

His words stung. And it was so unfair. I'd rather clean toilets than work in the gift shop. Okay, I wouldn't rather clean toilets. But still, it would be so boring in the gift shop.

"You know, there is, like, a major party happening on Sunday," I told him.

"The Spencers' party. Marci with an i. Yes, I'm aware of that."

"Am I going to help plan it?"

He cleared his throat. "I think Charlotte and Lisa are working on that. Your responsibility now is the gift shop."

He had always been so nice to me, but right now, he seemed mean, unreasonable even. I almost told him that I quit, but part of me wondered if that's what they wanted. Yes, knowing that Marci was coming to the park made me a little paranoid. Making me miserable seemed to be her purpose in life. But she didn't know I worked here, so maybe I *had* just taken it too far when I'd walked away from the parties on Wednesday. I angled my chin defiantly and stood up. "Okay."

I headed for the door, stopped, and turned around. "Did Charlotte tell you about my ideas for the luau?"

"Yes, but they're a little more than we want to do for this event."

"If you don't give Marci Spencer something special, she's not going to be happy. Trust me, you don't want an unhappy Marci."

"We'll take care of things."

The tone of his voice dismissed me as clearly as if he'd waved good-bye. I was once again tempted to call David, tempted to go home. It wasn't as though I needed the job. Besides, Dad was coming home this evening. I wanted to get an early start on spending some time with him.

But I didn't go home. Instead I headed on over to the souvenir and gift shop. The window display of the shop had sand along the bottom and a treasure chest on its side, with its top open and trinkets spilling out. Not bad. It looked like someone here actually had an imagination.

I walked inside. It was a large shop. The square counter with a register on each side was in the middle of the building. Four people were inside the center, each manning a cash register. I counted six people wearing Paradise Falls uniforms standing around the shop. I knew their jobs weren't so much to help customers as to make sure that none of them walked out with items that they'd "forgotten" to pay for. The park lost a lot of money because of shoplifting. I used to think that with most of the customers wearing bathing suits, shoplifting wouldn't be a problem. I mean, really, where were they gonna hide stuff? But they managed to make off with a lot. Maybe it was because people often came in here with their tote bags in tow.

A guy walked out of the back, spotted me, smiled, and hurried over. He was probably in college. He was tall and slender. I imagined that he could walk down the crowded aisles and never knock anything off the shelves.

When he reached me, he said, "I'm Zach. You must be Whitney."

"Yep. I'm here to help out."

"Great. Just walk through the store, keep an eye on the customers. Be aware of shoplifters."

"It really looks like you have enough people here," I told him.

"We never have enough. Never, never, never." He turned around and clapped, his hands held high as though he was about to start dancing. He was very dramatic. "All right, everyone, this is Whitney. She's going to help us out today."

I was really glad to hear the "today" part. Maybe that meant that today's assignment was temporary — as in Mr. T had gone temporarily insane to think that I was going to do this for the remainder of the summer.

The bells sounded, signaling the opening of the park. I strolled through the store, trying to look busy. Most people bought their souvenirs at the end of the day, although we also sold things that people usually forgot, like sunscreen, disposable cameras, and film. Of course, we charged double what people could buy the items for outside of the park. But there was no law against that. Quite honestly, absentmindedness came with a price.

An hour into my shift, I was totally bored. A couple of the employees said hi to me, but I was the new kid in a store that had way too many workers. Customers were scarce. We did have someone come in looking for a toothbrush. Why she needed to brush her teeth while she was at a water park was beyond me. We didn't carry toothbrushes. Oddly, we carried toothpaste. That, too, made no sense. I told myself that maybe the strange assortment of merchandise signaled I was needed here to get the inventory under control, but truthfully I just didn't care about all the little things we carried in the store.

Fearing that I was on the verge of dying of boredom, I walked over to the window and gazed out. A large smudge caused a glare, but I thought I saw —

I went to the door and peered out. It *was* Jake.

What was he doing in this section of the park with his ice-cream cart? Why wasn't he working the parties?

I glanced around the store. Zach wasn't anywhere in sight and we had two customers — teenagers looking at souvenir T-shirts. I walked out of the shop.

Jake grinned when he saw me. "Hey."

He was dipping ice cream for three young girls.

"What are you doing here?" I asked.

"Just a sec." He gave them their ice-cream cups, took their money, and dropped it into his cash drawer. "Now what?" he asked, turning back to me.

"What are you doing here?"

"Working."

I scowled at him. "I can see that. Why aren't you at the parties?"

"They rotated me out."

"You're kidding?"

"Nope. Looks like they rotated you, too." He scooped out some vanilla ice cream — my favorite — into a cup and held it out to me.

"I'm not on break."

"What are you doing out here then?"

"Just wanted to see what you were doing." I crossed my arms over my chest. "My getting rotated was not by choice. I'm hoping it's just temporary."

"This could be temporary, too. Who knows?"

I wondered if I went back to parties if he'd get rotated back over there. It was sure coincidental that we both got moved out of parties on the same day. Ice-cream carts were located all over the park. It was just a little odd that he was working a cart near where I was working. I couldn't help but think that Lisa had told him that I'd moved over here so he'd moved, too — to be closer to me.

If that was true, then maybe he really did like me in a romantic kind of way. But if that was the case, why didn't he kiss me last night? Why hadn't he held my hand more?

We'd done things together two nights this week, and I was no closer to figuring us out than I had been before.

"Interesting," Robyn said after I told her and Caitlin about Jake ending up working near me again.

We met at Tsunami but decided to have lunch at the food court, so we were sitting at a table, talking quietly because other employees were also taking their lunch breaks.

"I thought so," I said, and I couldn't stop myself from grinning. Even though I was still upset about not working parties, I was happy about Jake.

"Y'all sure do move around a lot," Caitlin said. "I don't know anyone else who moves around as much as y'all do."

"Not by choice," I told her.

"Do you want me to go defend you?" Robyn asked. "I mean, I was there, and I didn't think you did anything really awful. You were just trying to explain things."

"You'd do that?" I asked. "Defend me?"

"Sure."

"Have you never had any friends?" Caitlin asked. "Sometimes you come up with the weirdest questions."

"I've had friends," I admitted. "Just not like y'all."

"We have to stick together," Robyn said. "We don't want them to fire you."

"They won't fire me."

"How can you be so sure?" Robyn asked.

I thought about telling her and Caitlin the truth. But would they try to take advantage? It seemed like people were always trying to take advantage of me. I wanted to trust them. I really did.

Instead I said, "Let's go get an ice cream. My treat."

"Yeah, right, the park treats," Caitlin said, but she got up and followed me over to the cart where Jake was dipping ice cream.

We got in line behind the dozen or so people who were waiting. Half of them were park employees. I knew a couple of the people, the rest I didn't. The park had more than two hundred and fifty employees, so it was a little hard to remember everyone.

"Michael's meeting me after work. Do we want to do something together? All of us? You know the six of us?" Caitlin asked, twirling her finger in a circle like she was lassoing us all into her little web.

"Can't. My dad's coming in tonight. I want to spend some time with him," I told her.

"How about tomorrow night?" Robyn asked. "My mom bought a flat-screen TV. They're delivering it tomorrow, so I thought I'd break it in with a *Heroes* marathon. I can't believe Sean has never watched it. I'm going to rent the DVDs of the first season."

"Sounds like fun," Caitlin said. "I'll check with Michael."

Then they both looked at me. I felt like someone in a police interrogation room. "You want me to ask Jake?"

"Well, duh, yeah," Caitlin said. "You invited him to go get pizza."

"But shouldn't the next move come from him?"

She laughed. "You're acting like there are one, two, three steps to getting a boyfriend. Trust me, it's all random. You can't plan it. So sure, ask him."

"Well, it could get a little awkward. We've never actually gone out anyplace while my dad was at home. I can usually talk Aunt Sophie into anything. Dad not so much."

"Well —" Caitlin began, but I cut her off, because we were nearing the front of the line, only three employees in front of us. I didn't want Jake to overhear us talking about him.

"Don't say anything," I whispered.

"But this is a great chance for Robyn to invite him — very casually," Caitlin whispered back.

She had a point. That could work. Robyn could invite him and I'd just happen to be at her house. Uncomplicated. But it would still leave what he felt about me in doubt.

"OMG! Whitney, is that you?" The voice was nauseatingly familiar.

I spun around. Actually, everyone spun around. Marci Spencer just had that kind of cheerleader voice that got attention. The i's — Andi and Sandi — were with her. This was bad. This was so very bad.

They were wearing shorts and V-necked T-shirts. Each one was a different color, but so much alike that it was a little unreal. Marci's red hair was cut short. It fluffed out in all directions, reminding me of the downy feathers on a baby chick. She had streaked parts of it blue.

I thought about pretending that I was a doppelganger or a long-lost cousin who just happened to look like Whitney. I thought about a lot of things in those few seconds before Marci spoke again.

"What is with that outfit?" she asked. "Are you, like, working here?"

"Pretty awesome, huh?" Caitlin said, before I could answer with some alternate version of the truth.

I knew Caitlin was trying to do the friend thing, but I was pretty sure that she'd never met anyone like Marci before. Marci ignored her, held up her camera, and snapped a picture of me.

"Why did you do that?" I asked.

"Blackmail."

"Why would you blackmail her?" Robyn asked.

Ignoring Robyn now, Marci told me, "We're here to meet with the party planners.

There are some very specific things I want for my party. To make sure they happen, you'll probably need to talk to your dad about some of them."

"Why would her dad care?" Caitlin asked.

"Well, duh, because he owns Paradise Falls."

CHAPTER EIGHT

If I thought I could fit into Jake's ice-cream cart, I would have climbed into it and pulled the top down. I could hear the employees whispering who'd been standing in line. I knew they were whispering about me.

"Your dad owns the water park?" Caitlin asked.

"You didn't tell them?" Marci asked. "Why would you keep that a secret?"

Because they would find a way to use it against me. Because Dad wanted me to have a taste of the real world, to be a real employee. Because I knew people would look at me differently if they knew the truth. They would either want to be my friends, hoping to score points or favors at the park or they'd resent my position and post mean things about me on the Internet.

I'd wanted anonymity. But I could already feel the truth spreading through the park.

"Now that I know you're here," Marci said, "I'll just give you a call if we have any problems during our meeting. Remember, I always get what I want."

She and the i's walked away. No one had told me that today's party planning meeting included Marci. For the first time, I was actually glad that I'd been reassigned for the day. Charlotte and Lisa were going to have a rough afternoon.

"Yuck. Is that the girl you were friends with?" Robyn asked.

"Yeah." I turned back to the ice-cream cart. It was now my turn. I wondered where the other employees had gone. Probably to spread the news. I was a legend. I had planned an employee get-together, been responsible for movie night, and arranged a laser light show for the Fourth of July. I'd done it all without my dad being there. But I knew everyone would think I'd managed to accomplish all these things because of who my dad was.

And in truth, I probably had. Today was the first day that anyone had ever questioned my actions, had turned down my ideas. Maybe Mr. T had been indulging me. Maybe he'd had enough.

I waited for Jake to say something about what Marci had said, but he just scooped out our ice cream — without me even telling him the flavors. We visited the ice-cream cart a lot.

But I wanted him to say something. I wanted him to say something mean about Marci. I wanted him to say something nice about me. I wanted to ask him what I should do. I wanted to know if he felt different about me now.

But I didn't say anything either. We were the silent couple, or at least silent. I still didn't know if we were anything other than park employees who sometimes did things together.

Robyn, Caitlin, and I went back to our table. I stabbed my little plastic spoon into the ice cream, over and over and over. I imagined it was Marci's camera finger, the one she used to push the button for her blackmail photos.

"*So what* if she posts on the Internet that you work here?" Caitlin said. "I don't see that it's blackmail material."

"She'll find a way to make me feel like it's a picture of me standing there in my underwear. I don't know how she does it, but she does. And it doesn't matter if you do what she wants or not; in the end, she always posts the picture."

"Soooo," Caitlin began, "your dad owns the park. Is that the reason that anytime you want anything it happens?"

"Of course not. It's because I have great ideas." And a great think tank in my dad. It was true that I always asked his opinion about the ideas, from a purely business standpoint — but I presented them, and I made them happen, hadn't I? The real world wasn't my dad telling people to make me happy.

Dad wanted me to work this summer. He wanted me to work here. At first I resented it, and when I was at Splash, I didn't help as much as I should have. I was a little embarrassed by my earlier attitude.

But now I really liked what I was doing. I liked working in P&E. I liked making sure that people were having fun. But I was there because I was good at it, because I had amazing ideas. Not because my dad owned the water park.

"Hey," Sean said as he sat beside Robyn. "Shouldn't you be finished with lunch by now?"

"Just like a supervisor, worrying about a few minutes," Caitlin said.

"I'm not a supervisor anymore," Sean said.

"Old habits."

"You're avoiding answering my question,

so I take it the answer is that you're going to be late getting back to work."

"Did you know Whitney's dad owned the park?" Caitlin asked.

Sean visibly stiffened, as though someone had just poked him.

"You did know," I said.

"You knew the truth about her and you didn't tell me?" Caitlin asked, clearly angry at her brother for keeping a secret, while I was focusing on the bigger issue. Sean had known that my dad owned the water park. He'd been really nice to me even though I hadn't been the best of employees in the beginning. Had he cut me slack because of my dad?

"I was sworn to secrecy," Sean said.

"By who?" I asked.

"TPTB."

The-Powers-That-Be. In other words, the bosses. But who did those bosses include? Did they include my dad?

"That is so lame," Caitlin said. "You should have told me, at least."

"What difference does it make?" Sean asked. "You're friends now. How did you find out about Whitney's dad?"

"Some girl who is going to have a major party here told us. She seemed to think it was important."

I knew the first time that Robyn asked me to have lunch with her and Caitlin was because Sean had suggested it. At the time, I thought he was being a nice supervisor, watching out for those who worked for him. Actually, the very first day I worked here, I had lunch with him. He asked me questions about what I liked, what I didn't. He'd taken a keen interest in me. Now I wasn't sure that his reasons weren't because of my dad.

"Why did you ask them to be friends with me?" I asked.

He gave me a hard stare, then sighed. "Because you were assigned to my section, and my orders" — he made little quote marks in the air — "were to make sure you were happy."

"They *ordered* you to make sure I was happy?"

"It's no big deal. That was two months ago. Who cares now?"

I knew it was silly to get obsessed with this, but I suddenly wanted to know everything. "Why Splash? Why did they assign me to Splash? Because it's so easy?"

"It may seem like it's easy, but watching little kids playing near water is a lot of responsibility," Robyn said, clearly offended that I found fault with Splash.

But Sean hadn't answered my question. He seemed to think that Robyn's answer was all I needed. But it wasn't.

"So it was just random that I was assigned there?" I asked.

"I really gotta get back to work," Sean said.

I recognized an escape when I saw it. I reached out and grabbed his arm before he could get out of his chair completely. "Please, Sean. I need to know."

He sighed and pointed to Robyn.

I shook my head. "I don't get it. *Robyn* was the reason I was assigned to Splash?"

"I don't get it either," Robyn said. "Why would my assignment make a difference?"

"Because we knew if there was a problem you'd know exactly what to do and wouldn't panic," Sean explained.

"They thought I'd panic?" I asked. Now *I* was insulted.

"Look, I don't know. All I know is that during our first supervisors' meeting, Mr. T asked who we would trust in an emergency to get the job done — meaning if someone nearly drowned. I said Robyn."

"Not me?" Caitlin asked, irritation in her voice.

Sean groaned. "I can't win here. I'm going."

"No, wait," I said, still clutching his arm. "Your answer to Mr. T's question was Robyn, so they put us together?"

"Yeah. And it worked out, didn't it? When the kid almost drowned, who did the CPR?"

Robyn. And when a kid almost choked on his hot dog, who did the Heimlich? Caitlin. What had I done? Nothing important.

Dad wanted me to experience the real world, but this wasn't the real world. Disheartened, I got up. "I need to go back to work."

"Look, it doesn't matter that your dad owns the park," Robyn said.

If only that were true. But I had a feeling it wasn't.

"So is it true that your dad owns the water park?" the girl, a gift shop employee, asked.

I was back in the Treasure Chest, walking through the store, keeping an eye out for thieves. It had been a pretty slow afternoon. I knew things would pick up just before the park closed. A lot of the guests had season passes and they weren't interested in the stuff we had for sale here. But some were tourists, here for only the day. They'd be by to pick out a souvenir: an I Survived T-shirt or a snow globe or plastic sea creatures or seashells or sand dollars.

I was thinking that I should buy an I Survived T-shirt, although my surviving my summer at Paradise Falls had suddenly become very questionable.

I looked at the girl. In the shop, everyone wore little name badges. I didn't know if it was because I was new or temporary, but I hadn't been given one. Hers read DAHLIA. Like the flower. She had short black hair and milk-chocolate skin.

"Yes," I finally said.

"Is that the reason you don't have to do anything around here?"

"Uh, excuse me, but I'm looking for shoplifters."

"Yeah, right, like that's real work. Must be nice."

She walked away. She was the fourth person to ask me about my dad. Why did the questions make me feel like a loser, like I couldn't do this on my own?

I went up to Zach. "I'm taking a break."

He looked like he wanted to protest — especially since I'd been back at work for only half an hour. Instead he said, "Okay, sure, whatever."

I guess he didn't want to upset me. Maybe he thought his job was at stake. Or maybe I *was* useless.

I went outside, walked over to the little rest area, and sat down on a metal bench. It wasn't very comfortable but it survived the elements. I was wondering how *I* was going to survive the truth that was spreading through the park. I watched people walking by, laughing with their friends. Why was I even here?

A shadow crossed over me. I looked over. Jake was holding out a cup of ice cream. "Everything always seems better after ice cream," he said.

"It didn't help earlier," I grumbled.

"This is special."

"Yeah, what's so special about it?"

"It gives me a reason to sit and talk to you."

"Do you need a reason?"

"Not really." He sat down and set the cup of vanilla ice cream in front of me.

"I'm being hard to get along with, aren't I?" I asked.

He shrugged.

I took a bite of the ice cream. It was soothing but not as much as having Jake sit down beside me.

"Bad day, huh?" he asked quietly.

"The worst. Guess you heard all that stuff Marci said."

"Marci? She the one with the designer friends?"

I laughed, peered over at him. "Designer friends?"

"Yeah, they kinda looked like accessories, like a Prada handbag or something."

"What do you know about Prada?"

"My mom's into fancy stuff. Said she'd rather have one really nice purse than ten so-so ones."

"I'm not sure that analogy works because I'm not sure Marci's friends are *really* nice."

"I was just explaining how I knew about Prada, not saying that group of girls was nice."

"They call themselves the i's." I explained how they worked.

"Man, brutal," he said when I was finished.

"They can be." I shook my head. "When I first started working here, I didn't want anyone to know I arrived in a limo, I didn't want anyone to know we were really wealthy. I told Caitlin all my stuff was knockoffs. They weren't. Then as I started to get comfortable around here, I let things slip. Now everyone knows my biggest secret."

As though to prove my point, two employees walked by. The girls put their heads together when they saw us and talked low.

"See?" I asked. "They're talking about me."

"You don't know that. They could be talking about me, saying how hot I am."

I laughed. "You think so?"

"Don't you? I'm pretty hot. Course, that could be because it's a hundred and three degrees today."

I laughed some more. Jake always made me feel better, even if he wasn't doing a lot of talking. That he was talking so much now surprised me, but also made me feel good. He knew when to talk to make the unhappiness go away.

"Your dad owning the park — I think it's cool," he said. "I bet you know all kinds of things about the park."

The good thing was that he'd been giving me attention before he found out that my dad owned the park. So I knew his being with me now had nothing to with the truth he'd discovered earlier. It made me feel good about him, about us.

"I know some things," I admitted.

He looked around, before settling his gaze on me. "So do you know Mr. T's real name?"

"Tzonkryzkewski."

"Bless you."

"What?" I asked.

"Didn't you just sneeze?"

I laughed. "No. That's Mr. T's name. Tzonkryzkewski."

He laughed, too. "Oh, wow, no wonder he goes by Mr. T. What other park secrets do you know?"

"I know they're going to build a new slide over the winter. I've seen the design. It's going to be pretty awesome. It's a bunch of corkscrew turns. I haven't decided what to name it yet."

"You get to name the slides?"

I felt myself blush. "I get to offer suggestions. They don't use all of them."

"That's awesome, though."

I smiled. "Yeah, I guess it is."

I should have known Jake wouldn't be bothered by the truth. What did it matter if my dad owned the park?

"Listen, Robyn invited me to her place tomorrow night to break in her mom's media room. She said you might need a ride. True?" Jake asked.

I had a limo at my disposal. When did I ever *need* a ride anywhere? Still, I'd rather ride with Jake than David.

"True."

"So can I give you a ride?"

He asked it like he thought I'd say no. How could he not know how much I liked him?

"I'd love for you to give me a ride, but I have to warn you. My dad's coming home tonight, which means you'll probably have to meet him tomorrow night when you come to pick me up."

"You make that sound like it's a bad thing."

"My dad is a little overprotective. He might make you take a drug test."

"Seriously?"

"Have you ever watched *Meet the Parents*? I think Robert De Niro's character was based on my dad."

"So I may have to take a lie detector test, too?"

"Not that bad. But you'd probably get a

lot of questions, so I understand if you don't want to go through that."

He shrugged. "I've got nothing to hide. Besides, I've taken a lie detector test before. No big deal."

"Why did you take one?"

"My dad gave me one when I was about eight. To show me how it worked and to show me that if I ever lied, he'd find out. So I'm a pretty honest guy."

An honest guy. But would he tell me the truth if I asked him if he really liked me? Or would he avoid answering? And how could I still doubt how he felt about me? We were going to do something else together. He was going to risk meeting my dad. He *had* to like me, didn't he?

"Okay, then," I said, smiling, really glad that he wasn't afraid of my dad. "But don't say I didn't warn you."

CHAPTER NINE

My dad was standing on the steps leading up to the front door when David pulled the limo to a stop in front of the house. I knew David had sent a message up when we were at the front gate. I didn't wait for David to come around and open the back door. I was out of the car and rushing up the steps before David had even gotten out of the car.

"Hey, Kitten," Dad said, smiling.

"Dad!" I knew I was too old for certain behavior, but I still leaped up to hug him. It worked because I was short and he was tall.

Laughing, he wrapped his arms around me, squeezing tightly. I wasn't upset with him about all that had happened at the water park. I hadn't lied on my employment application, because that would have been illegal and I'd gone to the park numerous times with Dad when he had meetings, so the staff, like Mr. T, knew me. I was pretty sure that the order to keep me happy had come from park management — not my dad. Dad wanted me to feel normal after my bad experience with Marci, so calling for special favors would have been against the purpose of his idea.

Dad set me down, put his arm around my shoulders, and led me into the house. "Tell me everything."

"Oh, there's so much."

We went into the living room. I sat on the sofa, my feet tucked beneath me. Dad sat beside me, stretching an arm along the back of the sofa. I got my blond hair from my mom, my green eyes from Dad. Dad's hair was brown, always fashioned in a business-cut style, never a strand out of place. His personal trainer kept him in shape, made sure he ate healthy. Unlike Aunt Sophie, Dad didn't do Wicked Wednesdays. He never strayed from his proper diet. Which I guess is admirable, but is also slightly boring. Especially when I'm the one sharing meals with him.

I told him all the good things that had happened at the park. When Dad first gets home from a trip, I don't usually lay all the bad stuff on him. My mom had taught me that — when you first see someone, share the good stuff. Because first impressions last the longest, and if the first thing you do is gripe, they'll stop coming around. Not that Dad would abandon me or anything. Mom was just trying to make a point. She was full of wisdom.

I really missed her sometimes.

It was later, while Dad and I were having dinner at a fancy restaurant with Aunt Sophie that I brought up my plans for Saturday night. I thought it was a good idea to mention them while Aunt Sophie was around to give Jake her seal of approval.

But I didn't need it. To my utter shock when I mentioned Jake, Dad was totally cool with him giving me a ride to Robyn's. Who would have thought? He did say that he expected Jake to come inside, no honking in the drive. But other than that, Dad seemed to think Jake wasn't a problem. Jake wouldn't even have to take a drug test.

Of course, the fact that he was an employee at Paradise Falls indicated he had already passed a drug test. They took safety pretty seriously there, and all employees — including me — had taken drug tests before getting hired.

I was feeling so good about Dad being okay with Jake that I decided not to bug him about Marci. Besides, she wasn't really my problem anymore since I wasn't part of P&E. I knew that if I told Dad about my abrupt move to souvenirs that he'd arrange for me to be moved back to where I really wanted to work. But I didn't want him interfering. I managed to get a couple of real friends on my own. And now, quite possibly, I was going to have a boyfriend. Jake would pass Dad's inspection — no problem.

The next morning, I was back at the Treasure Chest. I heard through the grapevine that a final meeting had been held to discuss the luau. We were going to have a bonfire, hire a local band, and have a laser light-show.

Caitlin was my source about the laser light-show, because they talked to her about talking to Michael to see if he could set something up on short notice. He could. He even knew a local band that was looking for a gig.

I wasn't bothered about not being included in the meeting, because it meant I wouldn't have to deal directly with Marci. She never sent me an invitation. And I was cool with that as well, because I wouldn't want to be at the party without Jake. Besides, we would both be working. The staff got paid extra for after-hours events so there was actually a good bit of excitement in the air around the water park.

Jake was still serving ice cream near the Treasure Chest but I was a little self-conscious now that we were going to get together that night, and he was going to meet my dad for the first time — and Dad was going to meet him.

Jake and I could be taking our relationship to the next level.

I could hardly wait.

"So you and David?" I asked Aunt Sophie.

She was in my room doing the whole makeup-so-it-doesn't-look-like-makeup thing. It was Saturday night and I was getting ready for what was almost a date. Usually she stayed at an apartment in the city when Dad was home, but she'd decided to hang around a few more days. I could think of only one reason for that development. She wanted to be close to the chauffeur.

"Is there more to that question? Because I'm not sure where it's going," she said.

"Are you two an . . . item?" I prodded.

"Uh, yeah. You have a problem with that?" She leaned back and looked back at me. She had green eyes like mine.

"No. I think it's kinda cool actually."

"Good."

"So how long have you been dating him?" I asked.

"Oh, about a month now." She tapped my forehead. "Don't bug your eyes like that."

"But how did I miss it?"

"We're very discreet."

"Does Dad know?"

"Not yet."

"I think he'll be cool with it," I assured her. "I mean if he was cool with Jake, he should be cool with David and you."

She furrowed her brow, looked like she wanted to say something, then shook her head as though she'd changed her mind.

The doorbell rang. Jake was here!

"Hurry up and finish," I told her, no longer interested in discussing David and her.

"Relax. You know your dad's going to want to talk to him."

"But I don't want him to scare him off."

"Who do you think is going to be doing the scaring?"

"Dad, of course. I don't want Jake to have to be alone with him for too long."

"Oh, all right," Aunt Sophie said, rolling her eyes and stepping back. "You're beautiful."

"Thanks, Aunt Sophie." I hurried to my bed and grabbed my tote. I looked back at my aunt. "If you get married, will I get to be a bridesmaid?"

"*If* I ever get married. Let's not rush this, okay? I just discovered I like him and we're taking it slow."

I rushed out of my room and down the stairs. I glanced around. No Jake. Had Dad run him off, just like I'd been afraid would happen?

I looked out the window. Jake's truck was

still there. I peeked into the living room. Empty.

Then I realized where they'd be. Dad's library. He always met with people in there. It was his favorite room. He always had business meetings there, and even though this wasn't a business meeting, I had a feeling that he'd treat it like one.

I felt a little like Caitlin because I was feeling nosy. I wanted to know what they were talking about, what they might be saying about me. Specifically, what Jake might be saying. This could be the moment I'd been waiting for, when I found out what he really thought of me.

Was he telling Dad how much he liked me? Was he explaining that he wanted us to get serious?

I knew what Dad was saying — that I was his princess and he'd do anything to see that I was happy.

As I neared the library, I slipped off my sandals so Dad and Jake wouldn't hear me coming. I crept to the open doorway. I peered around the corner. Dad was sitting at his desk, leaning back in his leather chair, looking calm and relaxed.

Jake was standing in front of Dad's desk, his hands stuffed into the back pockets of his jeans. Even from my angle, he looked like he was stiff, nervous. I'd never seen him nervous. He always seemed to be a guy in control.

"Jake —" Dad began, and his voice rumbled like it did when he was talking to a business associate. It was authoritative, left no room for arguing.

"I'm sorry, Mr. St. Clair," Jake said, obviously not recognizing the tone of Dad's voice. "But I can't keep taking money for being with Whitney."

I was surprised that they didn't hear my heart slam against my ribs.

I spun around and pressed my back to the wall. I could hardly breathe. My lungs just didn't want to draw in air. I thought maybe I was dying. I sure felt like I wanted to die.

From the very first day at the water park, I had noticed Jake, because I had spotted him watching me. All summer Jake had been there for me. He worked near wherever I worked. We started doing more things together. I had fallen for him — hard.

I thought he liked me. I thought he wanted to be with me because he liked me.

Only now I knew the truth.

My dad had been paying him to be with me. Dad had been buying me a boyfriend.

CHAPTER TEN

I slipped out of the house, knocked on the door of David's apartment above the garage, and told him that I needed to go to Robyn's. He didn't question me, probably because when Dad hired him he told him that he was supposed to take me wherever I wanted to go, whenever I wanted to go — as long as it was before ten o'clock at night.

He may have thought the black truck in the drive was unusual, but he didn't say anything about it.

I had him take me to Robyn's, because it was the only place I could think of that might offer me a safe haven. Not that I could hide out there. David would tell Dad where he had taken me if Dad asked him. After all, Dad was paying him, too.

On the way over to Robyn's, I called Aunt Sophie on her cell phone and told her what I had overheard. I also explained that I just needed some time away, was fine, was going to Robyn's, and wasn't going to do anything foolish.

Aunt Sophie understood. After all, Dad was her brother. She had known him her whole life and knew he liked to control things. But even she admitted that this time he had gone too far.

"Buying you a boyfriend? You can get one on your own. What was he thinking? He told me there was a guy at the park named Jake who might want to do things with you, and that it was okay for you to be with him, that your dad trusted him, but I had no idea he was paying him!"

Like that confession was supposed to make me feel better. It only confirmed what I had heard, and it explained so much, like why Jake's name seemed to mean something to her and why she'd been perfectly okay with me going out with him. Aunt Sophie probably would have gone on a little longer but I'd told her I was losing my reception.

When I got to Robyn's, she, Caitlin, Sean, and Michael were already there, waiting to start the party, waiting for Jake and me to get there. Only there would be no Jake.

Now they were all sitting around on the couch or a love seat, united, while I sat on the floor feeling so very alone. I knew those feelings weren't fair to them. But everything made sense now.

The reason Jake always seemed to be working wherever I was. The reason he hadn't kissed me.

"I thought he liked me. But my dad hired him. All this attention he was giving me was because my dad paid him to pay attention to me." My cell phone rang. I ignored it.

"So what — your dad staked out the water park, noticed who came and went, then hired Jake?" Caitlin asked.

"He owns the water park, Caitlin. He could have looked through all the applications and picked the person he thought would be best. Or maybe he took out an ad. Who knows? Jake's dad is a cop so maybe my dad thought Jake had the serve-and-protect gene. I don't know. I just feel betrayed by Dad *and* Jake."

Another cell phone rang. Not mine. Sean, looking sheepish, took his cell phone out of his pocket and looked at the display.

"I have to take this." He stood up and started walking to the far side of the room while flipping open his phone. Then he started talking really quietly.

I concentrated on him as a really awful thought started to form.

Robyn reached across and touched my knee. "Go on. Finish explaining."

"In a minute."

She looked over her shoulder at Sean. "He won't mind."

"Who do you think he's talking to?"

She shrugged. "I don't know."

"I think he's talking to my dad."

"You're just getting paranoid now," Caitlin said. "Why would he be talking to your dad?"

"Because my dad knows people, knows things, and has contacts."

Sean closed his phone and returned to sit by Robyn on the couch.

"Were you just talking to my dad?" I asked Sean.

"Yeah. He wanted to know what was going on and if you were okay. I said you were fine."

Typical guy. I wasn't fine. Couldn't he see that? Or maybe it was just that right now I was upset with all guys.

"Why did he call you?" I asked.

"Because he was worried."

I shook my head. "No, I mean why *you*? How does he know who you are? Was he paying you, too?"

"No. Absolutely not. Although he may have known I was your supervisor, because he talked to me about you working in my section of the park."

Great. Was there any part of my life that my dad hadn't tried to control? I looked at Michael. "So did my dad pay you to come to the water park, introduce yourself to me, and sell me on a laser light show that he'd already paid you to put on?"

He looked at Caitlin, looked back at me. "What?"

"Now that I'm thinking about it, you being at the water park and telling me about your dad's light-show company, and a customer canceling on the Fourth of July just seems way too coincidental all of a sudden."

"You think your dad manipulated things so you would get credit for bringing an amazing laser light show to the water park?" he asked, his voice echoing incredulity.

Was that what I thought?

"Talk about your conspiracy theories," he went on. "First of all, you came over to me —"

I held up my hand to stop him from going on. He was right. So many different things had happened about the light show. My dad couldn't have been responsible.

"I'm sorry. I'm doubting everything I know right now," I told him.

"Not our friendship, I hope," Robyn said.

"No, that's the reason I'm here. I trust you guys." They had been stunned to learn that my dad owned the park. Thinking back on it, Jake hadn't even questioned it. Now I knew he wasn't surprised because he already knew. Like his dad, he'd been working undercover.

Sean's cell phone rang again. He looked at the display and said, "Jake." He answered, talked for a minute, then lowered his phone. "Jake wants to know if he comes over whether you'll talk to him."

"No."

"He says he can explain."

Shaking my head, I fought back the tears. What was there to explain? I knew the truth.

Sean talked into his phone. "Maybe another time, dude." He hung up and looked at me. "What now?"

"I don't know."

I got up, took a couple of steps toward the door, walked back. I had nowhere to go and no way to get there. I had told David to go on back home. So here I was. In a pinch, I figured Sean could take me somewhere, but again, I had nowhere to go.

I was mad at my dad for thinking he *had to pay* a guy to be with me, and I was angry at Jake for *taking* money to be with me. Was I really such a pathetic loser? Did my dad think I couldn't get a boyfriend on my own? Did he think he had to buy everything for me?

I just wanted to curl into a ball and cry.

"Do you want to spend the night?" Robyn asked, like maybe she knew what I was thinking.

"Would it be okay, do you think?"

"Absolutely."

"Your mom wouldn't mind?"

"Of course not. We don't have any plans."

"I didn't bring any clothes."

"I've got some stuff you can wear. It'll be fun. We'll have a sleepover."

I called Aunt Sophie. She gave me permission to spend the night. She also said that Dad was upset that I heard him and Jake talking. He never meant for me to find out that he was paying Jake to "look after me." According to Aunt Sophie, those were the exact words he had used. My conversation with her didn't make me feel any better. It only confirmed that Jake had been hanging around me because my dad had paid him to.

I felt like such a loser knowing my dad — *my dad* — thought he had to pay a guy to be my friend. *"Here's five bucks. Hang around with my daughter."*

Only knowing my dad, knowing how much money he had, I figured he had paid Jake way more than that.

And for Jake to be working wherever I was working, to always be in sight of me, the people in management had to have been in on it. They knew what Dad was doing, that he was paying Jake to hang around with me, so they made it easier for him to be wherever I was. It was a conspiracy, a conspiracy to ruin my life.

I didn't think I could ever show my face at the water park again. I knew how gossip worked, and while this secret had been held tightly, I knew it would come out eventually. I didn't want to be around when it did.

After Caitlin and the guys left, Robyn took me up to her room. It was really different from mine. Smaller, for one thing, but it still had space for two twin beds.

"Caitlin spends the night a lot," Robyn said as though she wanted to explain the beds.

All the furniture was white, and the room was painted yellow. It was like stepping into sunshine. She had pictures of actors and bands — obviously the torn-out centerfolds from teen magazines — stapled to her wall. All the art on my wall was framed and original.

Her room looked and felt lived in. Mine was like a showroom. I never really realized that before.

"Here. You can sleep in these." She handed me pink cotton shorts and a white tank top with pink flowers on it.

I went into the bathroom and changed into them, even though I didn't think I'd do a lot of sleeping. I figured I was going to spend most of the night brooding.

I don't know how long I stayed in the bathroom wondering about my next move. I knew I couldn't stay at Robyn's house forever, but I didn't want to go home either. And I certainly wasn't going to work. Maybe I'd stay with Aunt Sophie in her apartment. Maybe she could adopt me.

When I finally left the bathroom, I was surprised to see Caitlin sitting on one of the beds with Robyn. Both were in shorts and tank tops.

"What are you doing here?" I asked Caitlin. Hadn't she just left?

"You don't think you and Robyn are going to have a sleepover and not invite me, do you? I just had to go home and get my stuff."

That's when I noticed the large tote bag on the floor by the bed.

I guess I was surprised that Caitlin was there, but glad, too. At a moment like this, I needed friends. I sat on the other bed, with my legs tucked up beneath me, facing them. "Now what?"

"Well, we used to talk about boys —" Robyn began.

"Until she started dating my brother." Caitlin held up her hands. "I don't want to go there. Tonight we're here for you. What do you want to do?"

"Truthfully? I just feel like crying."

Caitlin reached across Robyn and grabbed a box of tissue that was on the nightstand. She tossed it at me. "Have at it."

I smiled sadly. "I haven't cried since my

mom died. Talking to my aunt about boys — it's just not the same."

"So talk to us," Robyn said.

She made it sound so simple, so honest. I was used to everything being complicated, and looking for ulterior motives. But with her and Caitlin, maybe I could simply tell the truth.

"I really liked Jake a lot."

"I don't get why he was taking money to be with you," Caitlin said. "I mean, at Pizza Palace, it looked like he was totally into you."

"He was just pretending." It hurt to say that but I knew it was the truth. Just like Marci had pretended to be my friend. I had shared my life with her and she had plastered it on the Internet and sold it to a gossip magazine.

"What if he wasn't?" Robyn asked.

"I know he was taking money because I heard —"

"No. What if he wasn't pretending? What if he did like you? Maybe the money was for something else."

"I don't think so. I know what I heard. And if I was wrong? When I called Aunt Sophie, she would have told me to come home."

"So what are you going to do?" Robyn asked.

I flopped back on the bed and stared at her ceiling. At home, I would be staring at the canopy of my bed. My room was designed for a princess. Right now, I didn't feel like a princess. I felt like someone in need of a fairy godmother. But those existed only in fairy tales.

"I'm not going to work tomorrow," I said, my mind made up. "I may never go to the water park again."

"You'll have to call in with an excuse," Robyn said.

She was a rule follower. I rolled my head to the side and looked at her. "What do you think they'll do? Fire me."

"They might."

"Yeah, right. And even if they do, so what? I'm probably going to quit anyway.

Besides, they won't even notice that I'm not there."

"Sure they will," she insisted.

I sat back up. "I'm inconsequential. I'm a token employee. You heard what Sean told us earlier today. They put me at Splash because they knew if there was a problem, you'd take care of it. You saved a kid. Caitlin saved a kid. I took pictures at parties. How important is that?"

"You give people memories, and you come up with awesome ideas," Robyn argued. "Like the laser light show for the Fourth of July."

I shook my head, doubting everything. "They did it because of who my dad is. Who knows if it was really a great idea?"

"People loved it."

"Maybe. I guess." I shook my head and lay back down. "Tomorrow is Marci's party. I don't want to be there. Can we talk about something else?"

Avoiding my problems seemed like a really good idea at the moment. Somehow

I had fallen into an alternate universe where I was living the year that nothing went my way.

Robyn didn't want to talk boyfriends, because she felt funny talking about Sean with his sister. Caitlin didn't want to talk about Michael since Robyn and I weren't talking about guys. So we talked about how in just a few more weeks, summer would be over and we'd all be going to school again.

I thought about the private school I went to. I had always liked it there until the i's had betrayed me. I wasn't looking forward to going back. I wanted to go to the same school as Robyn and Caitlin. Of course, that meant going to the same school as Jake. And I wasn't certain that I wanted to do that.

Although I was talking big about not going back to Paradise Falls because I didn't want to run into Marci, the truth was that I was avoiding Jake.

How could I possibly look at a guy who had been paid to be with me?

CHAPTER ELEVEN

The next morning, I was the first one to wake up. I slipped out of bed and nearly stepped on Robyn, who had spent the night sleeping on a mound of blankets on the floor. She reminded me of a kitten curled up there.

I knew I couldn't hang out at her house all day. I was going to have to go home and face my dad. In the harsh light of morning, my reaction seemed a little over the top. I should have faced Dad and Jake right then and there in Dad's library last night. I shouldn't have run.

I didn't think Robyn would have run. Caitlin, for sure, wouldn't have run.

Dad wanted me to learn about the real world. That meant facing things that I didn't like.

I sneaked out of the bedroom. I had left my cell phone downstairs. My plan was to get it and give Aunt Sophie a call. She would come and get me. Maybe she could help me decide my next step.

But when I got downstairs, I heard voices. Robyn's house was small enough that the voices carried out of the kitchen. One of the voices was really deep. I recognized it immediately. It was my dad.

I walked to the kitchen doorway. Dad was sitting at the counter talking with Robyn's mom. They each had a mug of coffee. The mugs didn't match. It was an odd thing to notice, but I did. Just like I noticed that they were smiling at each other as though they knew each other.

"Great," I said from the doorway. "This is just great. Tell me you didn't pay Robyn and Caitlin to be my friends."

Dad jumped off the bar stool as though

I'd caught him doing something he wasn't supposed to be doing. "Of course not," he said. "I thought you'd be ready to come home this morning, so I came to get you. And met Ms. Johnson."

"Like I'm supposed to believe that."

Dad didn't get after me for the sarcasm dripping from my voice. Normally he would have, but I figured right now he was feeling guilty that I'd discovered the truth. I could probably get away with a lot if I wanted. But I didn't want to.

"Why don't you get your things and we'll discuss this at home?" Dad suggested.

I wasn't sure if I was ready to discuss it, but I didn't want to be a burden to Robyn's mom either. I knew I was being difficult. Dad would get embarrassed and angry. Then I'd get angry and hurt. He was right. The best thing to do was to go somewhere else to discuss it.

I went to the media room where I'd left my tote bag the night before. I grabbed it, then went upstairs and changed into my clothes.

Apparently the Johnsons had company a lot — or maybe they just liked being hospitable — because they had a little basket with unopened toothbrushes and toothpaste and all sorts of little travel things like you'd find in a hotel. I brushed my teeth really quickly and did what I could to feel halfway human.

When I came out of the bathroom, Robyn was standing near the door.

"Your dad's here," she said.

"Yeah, I know."

"What are you going to do?"

"Go home."

"Are you going to come to work today?"

"No." As a matter of fact, I probably wasn't going to go back ever again. What was the point? It wasn't the real world. I was just playing at working, doing what I wanted to do. Everyone else carried the responsibility. Everyone pretended that I worked, and watched to pick up the slack when I didn't.

"I'm sorry if you had to work harder at the beginning of the summer because I wasn't doing my job," I said.

"Puh-leez! I stood around and watched kids slide. How much work is that?"

I was embarrassed to admit it, but I said, "Sean was right. I couldn't have done the CPR. During class, I did just enough to get certified and then I forgot it all. I thought it was stupid, that I'd never use it. No one had ever drowned at the park before."

"Don't keep beating yourself up about it. It's over."

But it was the same at P&E. I had ideas, but Charlotte and Lisa made them happen.

"I'd better go. Dad is waiting." I headed for the stairs, stopped, and turned back around. "It was really weird, the way your mom and my dad were talking. Like friends. Are they, do you think?"

Robyn shook her head. "I don't see how they could be. But Mom always tries to make people feel welcome."

I nodded. She was probably right. That's all it was.

When I got downstairs, Dad was waiting by the door with Ms. Johnson.

"Ready, kiddo?" he asked.

"Yeah." I thanked Ms. Johnson for letting me spend the night.

"You're welcome," she said. "I hope you'll come back."

It was weird — the way she smiled at me, then smiled at Dad. The smile she gave him seemed brighter, more inviting. I knew Robyn's dad wasn't around, had left her mom years ago. Still, I didn't want to think about my dad dating anyone. Not yet. Maybe never.

Finally, we were finished with our goodbyes, and Dad and I were heading home with the top off his black Lamborghini. I had tried to talk him into a red one, but he wanted black. So Batman-ish.

"You hungry?" he asked.

I hadn't really stopped to think about it. I looked over at him. He was wearing sunglasses. The wind was lifting his dark hair. I wondered if Ms. Johnson thought he was attractive. He was. No doubt about it. He took good care of himself, except for all the hours he worked.

"Yeah, I am."

Dad pulled into the parking lot of a pancake house.

It wasn't until Dad had his coffee and I had my orange juice that he said, "Can I explain now?"

I guess he figured I wouldn't go ballistic in a public place. He was right. I did have some pride. After what Marci had done to me, exposing my private moments to the world, I wasn't going to do anything embarrassing with witnesses around.

"What's to explain?" I asked. "You paid Jake to be my friend."

Dad shook his head, took a sip of coffee, and grimaced. I didn't know if it was the coffee or his conscience that he'd reacted to.

He sighed. "Ever since we lost your mother, I've worried, not only about you getting hurt physically, but emotionally. When Marci hurt you, I felt bad that I hadn't been able to do anything to prevent what happened. I want you to be safe from all hurts."

"Even I know that's impossible, Dad."

"You're right. It is. But I know there are a lot of kids at water parks, a lot of older kids. Parents drop them off, and no one watches them. And I worried that there might be some bullies and that they might give you a hard time. I also worried that if any employees found out that your dad owned the park, they might get ugly. So, yes, I paid Jake to make sure that no one upset you."

I crossed my arms over my chest. "So he doesn't work for the park."

"No, he works for the park. They just know that wherever you're assigned, he's assigned. And I pay him extra."

"How much extra?"

"A hundred dollars a week."

Jake must have found watching me to be quite a burden to give that up.

"But he doesn't want me to pay him anymore."

"Because he doesn't want to watch me."

Dad cleared his throat, sipped his coffee, set the mug down, and tapped the handle. "I think there's more to it than that. You

203

should probably talk to him when you get to work."

The waitress set our plates of food in front of us.

"I'm not going to work," I said as I poured syrup over my chocolate chip pancakes.

"What? It's your day off?"

"Nope. I quit."

"You can't do that, Whitney."

"Yes, I can. It's a free country."

"I don't think that's a good idea."

"Yeah, well, Dad, neither is paying a guy to watch out for me. I'm not a kid anymore. Besides, it's not the real world. Everyone pretended what I did was important because they didn't want me to get upset. They figured if I was unhappy, you'd be unhappy." I felt tears sting my eyes and blinked them back. "It wasn't real, Dad."

None of it was. Not my job. Not Jake liking me. Maybe not even Robyn and Caitlin being my friends.

CHAPTER TWELVE

"Are you sure you won't be needing my services today, Miss Whitney?" David asked. He was usually so stern-looking, but now he seemed relaxed in his Dockers and polo shirt.

I was stretched out on the lounge chair by the pool in my backyard — taking in the sun, doing nothing, trying not to think about everything that was probably going on at Paradise Falls. It was Sunday and the place would be packed. We closed at seven on Sunday, which would give the party planners an hour to get things ready before Marci and her gang showed up for *the* event of the summer.

I peered up at David. Aunt Sophie was standing beside him. They were holding hands. Aunt Sophie looked so happy.

"I'm sure," I told David. "I'm not going to do anything but stay here all day."

"What about that big party that was being planned for tonight?" Aunt Sophie asked.

"They can handle it without me."

"Are you sure —" David began again.

"I'm sure." I waved my hand. "Go to a movie or something."

"Okay," Aunt Sophie said as she leaned down and kissed me on the forehead. "If you're sure you'll be all right."

"I'm fine." All I wanted was to be alone.

As I watched them leave, I thought sadly, *At least someone in this family is experiencing romance.*

My little dog, Westie — who happened to be a Westie — came over, put his paws up on the end of the lounge chair, and started licking my bare toes. I should have been happy. I had no responsibility. I didn't have to deal with moms who thought their kids weren't getting enough attention. I didn't have to search for more party favors. I didn't have to help Jake scoop ice cream when there were so many kids wanting some that he couldn't keep up. I didn't have to help dads figure out how their new digital cameras worked.

It was strange, lying there, realizing all the different things that I took care of. Charlotte always said that our job was to put out fires. Not literally, of course. But whenever a problem arose, we were the ones who were supposed to take care of it. Any way that we could.

So I'd taken care of little things, put out little fires. But I hadn't saved any lives, hadn't done anything worth remembering.

A few hours later, I heard the sliding glass door that led onto the patio open. Westie went to investigate. I knew it was Dad, and Westie knew Dad was always good for a little petting.

"You've got a phone call," Dad said, holding the cordless phone out to me.

I couldn't imagine who it might be. Anyone who might have called me would have called on my cell phone. Plus, anyone I wanted to talk to was at Paradise Falls, working. Of course, I guessed that Robyn or Caitlin could have been taking a break.

I took the phone from him, gave him a pointed look, and waited until he walked away. Then I put the phone to my ear. "Hello?"

"Whitney, it's Charlotte."

The next-to-the-last person I wanted to talk to, Jake having the honor of being the *very* last person I wanted to talk to.

It was nearly time for the park to close. Had she just realized that I hadn't come in? And why would she care? I was working in souvenirs now.

"First of all," Charlotte said, "I want to apologize about the whole mix-up that resulted in you being sent to souvenirs."

Even though I wasn't there, they were still trying to make me happy. They were afraid of Dad. "It doesn't matter, Charlotte."

"I don't think Lisa realized how much you really do. I know I didn't."

I was close to gagging. "Seriously, Charlotte, you don't have to do this. I'm quitting. I'm not coming back, so none of this matters anymore."

"You can't do that."

"Uh, I think I can. I mean, what are you going to do — fire me?"

Really, what could she do? Her options were pretty limited. Actually, her options were none.

"No, seriously," she said, "we need you."

"And I need to work on my tan."

"Look, Whitney, Lisa had a family emergency. Her grandmother's in the hospital, so right after the last birthday party today she went to be with her. I've got no one in charge of that stupid luau tonight. . . . I need you to come in."

"How much did my dad pay you to do this?"

"What?"

"Look, Charlotte, I know the entire

summer has been a scam. Everyone's been watching my back, making sure that I was given tasks I could handle all by my little self, and that someone was always there to make sure I didn't goof up. So good try. But I know as soon as I get there, Lisa's emergency will be over. She'll come back and I'll get pats on the back for saving the day — when I really didn't do anything." I was on a roll, trying to explain what I knew was going on. Dad and I were going to have to have another talk. He couldn't keep doing this; he couldn't keep arranging my life!

"I don't know what you're talking about," Charlotte said.

"My dad paid you to have an emergency. I'm not buying it. Bye."

"What? Wait —"

Only I didn't wait. I hung up as though she was an irritating telemarketer.

And now I was mad at my dad all over again. I got up and walked into the house. I found him in his study, looking over the designs for a new water park. He had three

TVs turned on, one to CNN and the other two on baseball games. He looked up when I walked in.

"Good try, Dad," I said. "But I'm not falling for it again."

"What are you talking about?"

"Paying Charlotte and Lisa to have an emergency so I'd feel needed."

"Want to explain *exactly* what you're talking about?"

I told him about Charlotte's call and Lisa's "emergency."

Leaning back, he tapped his Montblanc pen against the edge of his desk. "Whitney, paying Jake to watch over you didn't disrupt the management of the park. He could do his job while doing what I was paying him to do. Paying someone to create an emergency situation, putting a burden on others so you can feel important? As much as I love you, Princess, and want you to be happy, I'd never do that."

As I listened to him, I realized how silly I'd been. Of course he wouldn't pay someone to have an emergency. He wouldn't do anything to put Paradise Falls at risk for not living up to its reputation of being the best water park in the area, or in the state. Our park had been featured on documentaries about the top ten best water parks in the world. What was I thinking to walk out, to quit, to leave them shorthanded?

"Can you drive me to work?" I asked.

Dad grinned. "Which car should we go in?"

When I got to the water park, I went to Charlotte's office. She was leaning over her desk, studying diagrams and notes. She looked up when I walked in. "Thank goodness. It's chaos around here. What does this mean?"

She pointed to a small X in front of Tsunami.

"That's where we're going to put the fire."

"Right." Her brow furrowed. "Where's the wood coming from?"

"You don't have the wood yet?"

"No. As she was heading out the door, Lisa said something about not having everything ready, but she was so worried about her grandmother that nothing made sense." She held up her hands. "I know I should have been paying more attention to the plans. I just expected y'all to take care of it. Y'all do the work. I get the glory."

I smiled. "You'll still get the glory."

"Right. Have you *met* the Spencers? They've been calling every hour to make sure that everything is good to go — even though I've been telling them that we couldn't start to get things ready until the park closes."

The receptionist peered inside the room. "A guy is here. Says he needs to know where to set up the *laser light show*?"

I couldn't stop myself from smiling; even when she told us something, she made it sound like a question, like maybe she wasn't sure why he was here.

"Yeah, that's Michael. The band is going to set up on one side of Tsunami. Are they here yet?"

"No?"

I looked at Charlotte. "I'm going to need some people to help me."

"Get whoever you need."

"Can I have Lisa's list?"

"Sure, but I don't know how you can read it."

She handed it to me and I looked at Lisa's notes. Most of them were abbreviations like what I used when I text-messaged. How old was Charlotte anyway not to be able to figure these abbreviations out? The clambake was a no-go, but I saw notes for a lot of the other things that I'd suggested.

"Charlotte, do you know where the leis are?" I asked.

"In the storage room."

"Would you be okay taking them to the front gate so we can pass them out to people as they come through?"

"Good idea. What are you going to do?"

"Take care of everything else."

Then I went to find my very special team.

I went down the hall to the marketing office and stuck my head in the door. Sean was working at his computer.

"I need you," I told him.

"Looks like you're here to work."

I guessed the fact that I was wearing my Paradise Falls uniform gave it away.

"Yeah, we've got the luau. I need you to find Jake. Since he has a truck, I need you guys to locate some wood that we can use to set up a small bonfire near Tsunami."

"I'll get on it."

I was walking back down the hallway when he caught up with me and put his arm around my shoulders.

"I'm glad you're here," he said. "You know how to throw a party."

"Just wish I had more time to get this one ready."

"Whatever you need, you'll find people willing to help."

"Yeah, right."

"Come on, Whitney, your dad's paying them."

I scowled at him.

He grinned. "It's called a salary."

I pushed him away from me. "Very funny."

"Seriously," he said. "They'll help because they like you."

As we parted when we got outside, I wanted to believe his words, but I remembered some of the looks that I got yesterday — the last day that I'd worked. The truth was out. I guess I was going to find out if it made a difference.

I ran into Michael as I was heading toward Tsunami.

"Caitlin said you weren't working today," he said.

"I wasn't. Now I am."

"I'm glad. I liked working with you when we did the light show before."

I walked him over to the pool and showed him where we were going to set up the band. Things were going my way because they showed up while I was still talking to Michael. They were a local band, wanting to make it big. I explained where they were to set up. Michael was familiar with the area because he had worked with his dad on the laser light show that we'd had on the Fourth of July, so he took charge of not only the light show but the band setup.

"Thanks," I told him.

"Not a problem."

I noticed the lifeguards standing around at the first lifeguard station.

"Caitlin!"

She moved away from the crowd. "I knew you couldn't stay away," she said. "I should have bet you another pair of shoes."

"Like you would have let me pay for them."

"You never know. Maybe I would have."

I didn't think so. "I could really use your help here," I told her.

"Sure. Just tell me what you need."

"We need to move all the lounge chairs and tables back some so we have more room for a beach. And when Sean and Jake get back with the firewood, I need you to help them get it set up in the middle."

"Are we going to party afterward?"

"No, not tonight. But I have an idea brewing."

"So spill it."

"Later. We gotta get this done."

"We'll take care of it." She pointed to the group of lifeguards behind her.

I left them to create the beach atmosphere that we wanted.

I knew as soon as the park closed that the Kiddie Zone crew would start barricading off their section because it wouldn't be open to our guests. I headed over to that area of the park. I saw the lifeguards and ride attendants putting up metal barricades. A couple of people would stand guard to make sure no one entered the forbidden area, but the rest of the crew would help us take care of the party guests. I asked a few of them to go to the front gate and help Charlotte. If enough people helped her, maybe she could even get out of lei duty.

Robyn spotted me about the same time that I spotted her.

"Hey!" she called out and hurried over. She hugged me. "I'm so glad you're here."

"Why?"

"Because people have been asking about you. They think it's cool that your dad owns the park and that you've been working with us all summer."

"Really?"

"Yeah. So are you here to help with the luau?"

"Pretty much. I need you to do something for me. Come on."

We walked over to the main pavilion we used for birthday parties. I took her back to the storage unit where we kept all the little party favors. I opened the door.

"These are for little kids," Robyn said. "You're not thinking of using them for Marci and her group, are you?"

"No, but I saw something the other day . . . here it is." I held up the little treasure chest. It was like the one that I'd seen in the souvenir shop window. Only inside were fake gold coins. "Scatter these around the park. We'll tell the guests that each one is valued at a dollar. They can trade them in for a souvenir at the Treasure Chest." I'd gotten the idea from the skee-ball prizes.

"Ah, sort of a treasure hunt."

"Sort of. It's the best we can do on short notice."

If I had come to work today, I probably would have thought of something better. It was really silly for me to have stayed away.

"I'll take care of it," Robyn said.

"When you're finished, come to Tsunami. That's where the action will be."

And where Marci would be.

It was time to face my nemesis.

CHAPTER THIRTEEN

When I got back to Tsunami, everything seemed to be ready. A medium-size fire was burning in the sand, near the shoreline. Wood was stacked up on the side, wood we'd use to keep the fire going throughout the party — until it was all gone.

Jake was standing by the wood. I guessed someone, maybe Sean, had put him in charge of keeping watch over that aspect of the party. It seemed appropriate since he was good at watching things — me, specifically.

I didn't know what to say to him, so I just gave him a little wave and went to check on the band. They had everything they needed, so they started warming up.

It was eight o'clock. When it got dark, in another hour or so, Michael would begin the light show. It was going to be simple, nothing as extravagant as what we'd had for the Fourth of July, but I was pretty sure it would impress Marci. After all, how many people had a laser light show at their birthday party?

"There you are," Charlotte said, and came to a stop in front of me. She was breathless. "Thanks for sending people to help with the leis. They have two hundred people coming through the gate."

"The leis make it special, like being in Hawaii or something." I told her about the gold coins. They weren't real, of course, just fake. "We haven't told anyone anything yet, so if you don't want to let them have a value and be traded in for souvenirs, that's cool. They'll just be something they find."

"No, I like it," Charlotte said. "I'll make an announcement once everyone is in here.

If you'll keep an eye on things, I'm going to go collapse for a few minutes. I'll be glad when this party is over."

They had only rented the park for two hours. The party would end at ten. Then we'd have to clean up.

I watched as people started wandering in. Two hundred people. For the first time, I felt a little sorry for Marci. Did she think all these kids were really her friends?

"I think it all looks great," Caitlin said, coming up to stand beside me. "We definitely need another employee party."

"Last day the park is open. And it'll be better than this."

"All right! So does that mean you're back at work?"

"You know it."

"Good. It just wasn't the same without you. Now I better get to my lifeguard station."

She started to walk away, stopped, and looked back at me. "I Googled you, by the way."

"Traitor."

"Robyn and I would never do that, you know. Post embarrassing stuff about you on the Internet."

I nodded. "Yeah, I know."

"Cool."

She headed to her lifeguard tower, and I started walking around just to check on things.

"Whitney St. Clair, is that you?"

I looked over. It was Mrs. Spencer. She was holding a huge box. "Hello, Mrs. Spencer."

"I don't remember Marci inviting you."

Ouch! "She didn't. I work here."

"Oh. Well then, take the cake and put it on a table in that pavilion over there. I need to find some people to help serve it."

"I'll take care of the cake and finding someone to serve."

"Oh, great. Marci's dad is bringing the other cake in. Marci wanted a yellow cake and a chocolate cake. With this many people, I hope it's enough."

"I'm sure it will be. We'll cut small slices."

She was walking away before I finished talking. So typical of Marci's family. They were all that mattered.

Very carefully I walked to the pavilion and set the cake on the table. Then I took a deep breath. It didn't matter how much I had done, if I dropped the cake, everything would have been for nothing.

"Hey, Whitney," someone said and I turned to see Suzy, a girl from my school. "Haven't seen you all summer."

"I've been busy working here."

"*Working?* That doesn't sound like much fun!"

"Actually, it's been a lot of fun."

"Huh."

I guess she couldn't think of anything else to say, because she turned and ran toward Tsunami.

People were arriving, dropping off their stuff, and heading to the various slides. With so few people here, they'd probably be able to slide down them all before the night was over.

I was getting ready to check on things when I saw Mr. Spencer. He looked a little lost. Birthday parties probably weren't his thing. Like my dad, he was a businessman. But tonight he was a dad. And he was carrying another large box with the other cake. I figured he didn't know where to put it.

I walked over to him. "Hi, Mr. Spencer."

"Whit —"

He tripped, the box wobbled —

I lurched forward, grabbed it.

"Whew!" Mr. Spencer said. "That could have been a disaster."

"No kidding. I'll take it to the table for you."

"Thanks."

He walked away and I carried the cake to the table. Once I set it down, I started laughing.

What do you know? I finally saved something after all.

* * *

I tried not to let the saving of the birthday cake go to my head. I walked around, making sure that I avoided Marci. I had spied her at the pavilion. Her auburn hair was styled so it was big and fluffy. I wondered if she had given any thought to what was going to happen with her hair the first time she went underwater. She was wearing a white bikini, so I assumed she was planning to hit the water. The other i's — Sandi and Andi — were standing near her in white bathing suits. It was like she was ignoring them and they wanted to be noticed so badly. Had I really considered her a friend?

Slipping away before she noticed me, I checked to make sure everything was ready for the light show, and that the band was ready to go. I gave them the signal that they could start playing. Music blasted through the park. Shouts went up from the partygoers and some started dancing on the beach. Others raced off to hit the rides.

With so many people, it didn't seem like

a very personal birthday party. The tables in the pavilion were piled with gifts. I wondered if Marci would get anything that she actually wanted. I thought that if I had a birthday party here, I would tell people their presence was present enough. Really, what did Marci need?

The park was serving free hot dogs, so I went through the food court and made sure everything was going well there.

"Some people are complaining because we're only serving hot dogs," the supervisor at Scavenger's told me. "Think it would be okay if we served hamburgers, too?"

I couldn't believe he was asking me. "What's your opinion?"

"I'd rather eat the cost on the hamburgers than listen to a bunch of complaining. Have you met the birthday girl? She didn't think our buns were fresh enough. They were delivered this morning."

I wrinkled my nose. "Yeah, I've met her. Hold on." I took my cell phone out of my shorts pocket and called Dad. I explained the situation.

"Sometimes you have to pay a little more to keep customers happy. Do what you think is best," he told me.

I hung up and nodded at the supervisor. "Serve whatever keeps everyone happy."

He grinned. "Great." He turned to his staff. "We're going into full service!"

I would have thought they would grumble about having more work to do, but apparently they'd already had their share of dealing with unhappy guests, because they got right to work.

Charlotte's announcement about the gold coins had been met with a lot of whoops from our guests, so I stopped in at the Treasure Chest. The employees were busy.

Dahlia walked over. "Have you met the party girl?"

"Yeah, why?"

"She came in here saying that she should have free gold coins. That *she* shouldn't have to search for them. Is she seriously spoiled or what?"

I knew better than to talk badly about a customer — or a past friend — to someone I wasn't friends with.

"Sorry you had to deal with her. If she comes back, tell her to speak with management." I figured Marci wouldn't bother to do that. It was one thing to terrorize clerks. I didn't think she'd go after the bosses. But even if she did, they were paid way more to deal with problems.

"Okay, thanks." Dahlia turned to go, then turned back to face me. "I heard you didn't want to come in today but they made you, so I guess you don't get to do everything you want. Sorry about what I said the other day."

So not all rumors were accurate. No one *made* me come into today except me. Still, I accepted her apology and headed out.

All around the park the ice-cream guys were busy. Seeing them reminded me of Jake, keeping vigil by the fire, making sure it didn't go out.

The band was loud and their music filled the park.

Just before nine, they sang "Happy Birthday." As soon as they finished, Michael started the laser light show.

I could hear everyone oohing and aahing — just like they had on the Fourth of July. It was really impressive, and the lights could be seen from most areas of the park so the partygoers didn't have to return to Tsunami to enjoy the show.

I grabbed a trash can on wheels and started moving it through the pavilion picking up the paper plates and cups that people had left behind after they'd taken time to eat the cake. Paper scraps from Marci's gifts were all over the place. I couldn't believe how inconsiderate the guests were. They couldn't have stuffed the wrapping into a trash can as she opened the gift?

I bent down to pick up a plate. It was upside down and when I lifted it, I discovered the cake was squished into the pavilion floor. I tried to scrape it up with the plate. *Yuck!*

Suddenly, there was a brilliant flash of light. I looked up. Marci was standing there with her camera, gloating.

So much for avoiding her completely.

"A new picture for my MySpace page," she said. "Whitney St. Clair works as a janitor. What next?"

I stared after her as she walked away. My heart was hammering. The world was going to see me cleaning up squishy cake. What would they say? What would they think? Would they laugh at me?

Suddenly, I heard laughter — *mine*.

Was I really worrying over this? Who cared if I was picking up trash? I knew my real friends wouldn't. As a matter of fact, they would think posting the picture was as ridiculous as I did.

At eleven o'clock, the bells sounded and Charlotte announced over the park intercom system that the party was over and that everyone should leave the park.

I was pushing a trash cart through

Tsunami when I heard, "This park is so lame. The party was supposed to end at ten. They can't even tell time."

It was Marci. She was talking to the i's.

And I'd had enough. I walked over to the group. "You know, Marci, you're pretty ungrateful."

Andi and Sandi gasped as though a creature had just emerged from the pool.

"Your parents paid so much for this party that the management decided at the last minute that you should have an additional hour. All the employees have been working hard to make sure you have a good time. Working extra shifts is voluntary. Yeah, we get paid more for the extra hours, but do you think we *want* to work? We'd like to be out having some fun, too, you know. Instead we're here, listening to you whine about everything you don't like, while you and your friends trash the park. Paraphrasing Buzz Lightyear here, you're a sad, strange little girl and you have my pity."

I heard clapping. I looked over my shoulder. Caitlin and Robyn were giving me a thumbs-up.

"You're just jealous," Marci said.

My mouth dropped open. "Of what?"

"Of everything I have, and because we kicked you out of our group."

I looked at the i's, then I looked back at Marci. Maybe for the first time I was seeing them as they were. Nothing would ever make them happy. "You didn't kick me out, Marci. I walked out."

Then I spun on my heel and headed to where Robyn and Caitlin were standing.

"You told her, girlfriend," Caitlin said as she and Robyn fell into step beside me.

"I think I used to be like them," I murmured sadly.

"No, you weren't," Robyn said. "Not on your worst day."

I laughed softly, then settled into silence and thought about it. "But no one really depended on me."

"Are you kidding?" Caitlin asked. "Who did they call when Lisa had to leave? Who did people go to when a problem came up tonight?"

I thought about it some more. "Me?"

"You. The awesome party-girl."

She was right, but it was more than that. Even though I no longer liked Marci, I worked hard to make sure tonight was a success, and I finally understood why I worked so hard.

Because it was my job.

CHAPTER FOURTEEN

It took us almost an hour to shoo everyone out of the park. Another hour to clean up.

"You did a great job," Charlotte said to me later. "You better report to work on time tomorrow."

"I will. The souvenir shop needs me."

"Not as much as I do. You're back on my staff."

"Thanks. I'm going to start planning the employee end-of-summer party."

"Whatever you want."

I knew she said that because my dad owned the park. But I wasn't bothered by that anymore. I had proved something to myself tonight. I had done this. I made this party happen.

I was standing at Tsunami, where the water lapped at the shore. I said good-bye to employees as they walked by, thanked them for what they had done.

"See you tomorrow," Robyn said.

"Wait." I walked over to Robyn and Caitlin. "I just wanted you to know that I couldn't have done tonight without you." I grimaced. It sounded corny but it was the truth.

"We didn't really do anything," Caitlin said.

"It's hard to explain, but tonight I realized what real friends are. They believe in you. I'm really going to miss you when summer is over."

"So, transfer to our school," Robyn suggested.

"The public school is so big. It's a little scary."

"But we'll be there for you. It won't be bad. It'll be fun."

I just didn't know.

"I'll think about it. Anyway, I just wanted to thank y'all for being my friends."

"You don't thank friends for being friends," Caitlin said.

Still, she hugged me. Robyn came closer and then all three of us were hugging. They were the best. The real world.

After Robyn and Caitlin headed home, I waited at the water park, near Tsunami, while everyone left. The band. The light-show crew. The lifeguards. The ride attendants.

Then the lights started going off one by one. All over the park.

A few distant lights stayed on, so everything wasn't plunged into darkness. Mr. T walked out of the office building.

I watched as he headed toward the path that would lead to the gate. I guess he didn't see me standing there. That was fine. I wanted a moment alone in the park, just to absorb my sense of accomplishment.

I closed my eyes and listened. I could hear the water and the slight breeze. It was never truly quiet around here.

I dug in my shorts pocket and pulled out my phone.

"Need a ride home?" Jake asked.

I nearly dropped the phone. The only person I had avoided more than Marci was Jake.

"I thought you left."

"Nope. So how 'bout that ride?"

"Actually I was just going to call my dad to come get me."

"I can give you a ride."

"It's out of your way."

"Not as much as it'll be out of your dad's way."

Unfortunately, he had a point. I thought about arguing, but there was an easier way to handle this.

"Let me call my dad." I stepped away from Jake and dialed home. Dad picked up on the first ring. I didn't waste any time getting to the point. "Jake wants to give me a ride home. Say no."

"Think I'm going to have to say yes."

"Dad —"

"Whitney." He was using his don't-argue-with-me voice. Then he said quietly, "Princess, he returned all the money to me."

"What? What do you mean?"

"Last night when he was here, he gave me back all the money I paid him to watch you."

I was stunned. "Why?"

Dad laughed low. "Welcome to the real world. Some things are more important than money."

"Why didn't you tell me that before?"

"I thought you were too mad to really listen. We'll talk more when you get home. Let him bring you. I imagine he might want to talk to you first, though. So he can have an hour. But that's all."

Dad hung up before I could object.

"What did he say?" Jake asked.

I turned to face him. "He said I didn't have to be home for an hour. So do you want to go somewhere?"

"Yeah, I do. I want to go to a tropical island. Wait right there."

Jake disappeared into the darkness. I wondered what he was doing.

Then I heard the water lapping more forcefully against the shore and I realized that he had turned on the waves, so it would be like we were at a real beach.

I saw Jake's silhouette as he came nearer. He was holding something in his arms. I realized it was firewood.

He set the load down on the sand and began building a fire.

"Sit down," he said.

I sat. It was a warm night. I could almost imagine all the stars that were in the sky, although very few were visible because the distant light of the city was washing them out. But it didn't matter. I heard the roar of the ocean and that was enough to help me imagine I was on a beach somewhere on some island.

When Jake had the fire going, he sat by me. "I guess you've been to a real tropical island," he said.

"Yeah. Several. I travel a lot with my dad." I looked at Jake. "He told me that you gave him back all the money. Why?"

Jake stared in the fire for a while. Finally, he said, "Because it didn't seem right to take money for something that I liked to do. I liked watching over you. I liked spending time with you. I liked talking to you. But I wanted more. And I didn't think I could have it while he was paying me."

"What else did you want?"

He stopped looking in the fire. He turned his head and looked at me. I could feel the intensity of his gaze even in the near-darkness.

"I wanted to kiss you," he said quietly.

I swallowed hard. "He's not paying you now, right?"

"No, he's not."

"So, okay."

I saw him grin. "I like you a lot," he said.

"I like you, too. A lot."

He leaned nearer. I stayed very, very still.

His lips brushed over mine. So light, like testing the warmth of water before diving in.

He settled his mouth against mine, kissing me more firmly. I had waited almost all summer for this moment. It seemed so right. With the night surrounding us, the fire crackling, the waves washing over the shore . . .

Just the two of us at the water park, kissing, really *was* paradise.

EPILOGUE

There was anticipation and a touch of sadness in the air. We were all waiting to hear the clanging bells that signaled the park was closing. Only this time, it was the final closing of the season.

Summer was over. Most schools in the area would be starting next week. The summer employees who went to college would be heading off. The permanent full-time employees would be around, of course, to oversee the maintenance crews who worked during the fall and winter to make sure everything was ready to go for next summer.

The owner, my dad, approved letting the employees have free rein over the park once it closed. The front office assigned me to arrange things. I, of course, recruited the usual suspects: Caitlin, Robyn, Sean, Michael, and Jake. Michael arranged for us to have a small light show at midnight. We were going to show movies all night, using the back wall of Tsunami as our screen. The rides were going to be open. All the leftover food, ice cream, candy — anything perishable — was going to be made available to the employees. Jake and I were going to deliver anything that remained in the morning to a homeless shelter.

Jake and I had been dating since Marci's party. He was my official boyfriend now. I liked him a lot, so much, in fact, that I'd made an important decision that I was going to tell my friends about as soon as the park closed and we met up for the party.

The bells sounded. Guests began gathering up their things to leave. I was walking through the Tsunami area when I spotted some people still lounging near the water. With a sigh I went over to them. "Didn't you hear the bells? Park's closing."

Aunt Sophie smiled at me. "We thought we'd hang around for the employee party."

"You're not an employee."

"David is."

David grinned at me. He looked a lot younger when he was smiling, when he wasn't taking things so seriously. He still drove me around, but in a few more months I'd be getting my license. I had a feeling that Dad would find another position for him. Maybe he'd be Dad's bodyguard. Who knew?

"He's not a park employee," I pointed out.

"I've never been at the park at night," Aunt Sophie said. "We want to stay."

"Oh, all right. But only on the condition that I get to plan your wedding." They hadn't set a date, but I knew it was coming. Even now, the engagement ring he'd given her was reflecting the last rays of sunlight.

"It's a deal," Aunt Sophie said.

Walking away, I realized that I had become quite the bargainer.

It didn't take long for the park to go into party mode. I met up with the gang at the food court area. Jake had my burger and a plate of nachos waiting for me as I sat beside him.

"Sorry I'm late," I said. "I had a few things to check on."

"Is everything set up right?" Robyn asked.

"It's perfect."

"I can't believe this is our last night here," Caitlin said.

"I can't believe school starts next week," Michael grumbled.

"I'm excited about school starting," I said.

"Why?" Robyn asked. "You'll have to deal with the i's again."

"No, I won't. I'm transferring to a public school."

Her eyes widened. "Our school?"

"Yep." My life-altering decision.

"Awesome!"

I looked at Jake. He grinned at me. It wasn't avoiding the i's that had made me ask Dad to let me start going to a public school. I wanted to be with my friends and my boyfriend.

"Are you going to work here next summer?" Sean asked.

I shrugged. "I don't know. Dad's opening a new water park and they might need employees with experience."

"Where's it going to be?" Jake asked.

I wiggled my eyebrows. "Paris."

"Oh, my gosh! I'm so there!" Caitlin exclaimed. "Imagine the shoe stores. And the clothes! Oh, my goodness, the clothes!"

I was laughing so hard that I could barely eat. I didn't know if we'd go to Paris next year. But who knew?

If I'd learned anything this summer it was that all things are possible when you have true friends.

Take a sneak peek at the

first book in the

ONCE UPON A PROM

trilogy!

∞

"What's more pressing than planning the prom?" Nisha asked.

Tara gave her friend a serious look. "Hello? Were you not there shopping right next to me today? You know I'm a week behind schedule in the dress department and now I'm . . ." She paused to check her handheld. ". . . three weeks late finding a cute guy to form a meaningful relationship with before P-day."

"You've got to be kidding, Tara. You don't *really* have that on your checklist, do you?" Nisha asked. "I mean, we'll all have a great time no matter who we go with . . . or don't go with."

"It's the prom, Nisha," Tara said, nibbling on another fry. "I wouldn't kid." Especially since she knew what would happen if she showed up solo. Of course Nisha and Jordan would make the extra effort to include her, but as the night progressed the slow tunes would certainly outweigh the fast ones. Eventually Jordan and Nate would casually disappear for some alone time while Nisha and Brian remained glued to the dance floor, swaying and losing themselves in each other's eyes until the DJ spun out the last dreamy song of the night. And what would Tara be doing? She'd be feeling pretty awkward as she watched over her friends' sparkly evening bags — back at the table, alone. No, going to the prom stag was definitely out of the question.

"Maybe I should forget about the dress for now," Tara said. "What I really need to do is focus on finding the right guy."

To Do List: Read all the Point books!

By Aimee Friedman

- ❏ South Beach
- ❏ French Kiss
- ❏ Hollywood Hills
- ❏ The Year My Sister Got Lucky

- ❏ Airhead
  By Meg Cabot

- ❏ Suite Scarlett
  By Maureen Johnson

- ❏ Love in the Corner Pocket
  By Marlene Perez

- ❏ Hotlanta
  By Denene Millner
  and Mitzi Miller

Summer Boys series by Hailey Abbott

- ❏ Summer Boys
- ❏ Next Summer
- ❏ After Summer
- ❏ Last Summer

In or Out series by Claudia Gabel

- ❏ In or Out
- ❏ Loves Me, Loves Me Not
- ❏ Sweet and Vicious
- ❏ Friends Close, Enemies Closer

- ❏ Orange Is the New Pink
  By Nina Malkin

Making a Splash series by Jade Parker

- ❏ Robyn
- ❏ Caitlin
- ❏ Whitney

Once Upon a Prom series by Jeanine Le Ny

- ❏ Dream
- ❏ Dress
- ❏ Date